S0-BRR-817

WILDROOT

DUNCAN C. SCOTT

Knights
Press

Stamford, Connecticut

Copyright© 1989 by Duncan Campbell Scott

All rights reserved. No part of this work may be reproduced in any form without the permission of the author, except for short quotations used for review purposes.

Cover designed by Christopher Karukas©

Published by Knights Press, P.O. Box 454, Pound Ridge, NY 10576

Distributed by Lyle Stuart, Inc.

Library of Congress Cataloging-in-Publication Data

Scott, Duncan Campbell.
    Wildroot / Duncan Campbell Scott.
      p. cm.
    ISBN 0-915175-34-7 : $9.00
    I. Title.
    PS3569.C616W55 1989
    813'.52—dc19   88-32618
                                  CIP

Printed in the United States of America

To
David, Lalie and Bettie

PART ONE

"I began as a tomboy"
— Zsa Zsa Gabor

Somewhere a coyote is howling.

This fire is my only friend. Beyond its light, its comforting heat, there is only darkness. A wide plain of darkness and noise. A range of noises — some like breathing, some like ripping cloth — along the open range. Sometimes, rarely, something ventures too near my flame. And then I see the reflection of eyes. Glinting. Just for a second. Then gone. Inches from the back of my neck, perhaps, but gone from sight. Into the range of darkness.

I close my eyes and listen. My rough, unshaven chin rests against the leather of my chaps, grazing there across the rough material. I pull off my hat and run my fingers through the hair that hasn't been cut since Yuma.

There's something fine about the desert night. When life forms appear that are so hidden during the day. When the sun goes down and the deep desert knows nighttime, the only winter this landscape will ever know. Night is your friend, the time when you don't need to wrap a bandana across your face just to be able to breathe with all the heat and dust swirling. But night is your enemy, too, when every rustle is a scorpion.

My horse is nearby. I can hear his cough and sputter. I think of our long day's ride. And the ride of the day before and the days before that. That long fast ride out of Yuma. Sometimes a moment, sometimes an hour before the law. Stark, my horse, my Mustang stallion, raced with all the *wildness of his heart. Carried me to freedom, to darkness, to a world of night and fear outside the gaslit realm of Yuma.*

Yet Stark, in a very real way, created our need to run.

I haven't forgotten how he threw a shoe. How that took me into the blacksmith's shop. The man looked up at me, up and down at me, as he slammed the molten metal with his pounding hammer. How he wiped his face with the red cloth that he pulled from his pants. Wiped his face and naked chest. How his eyes looked back into mine as he led the horse into a stall.

How he soon lead me into a stall.

How the mayor came to get his horse, that ridiculous Palomino, at just the wrong moment, when I could not keep the groan from pushing past my lips. And then the rush, the running, the chase. I was glad only that the blacksmith believed in work before play, that Stark was well shod.

I couldn't help but think of it: better I'd robbed a bank. Then I could understand being chased. Then I'd have something to show for it.

Somewhere in remembering, I'd stretched out on my back, clenched my arms tight across my chest. I could feel my taut muscles. Smell my sweat. I looked up at the stars overhead, their light twisting and folding the night sky.

I heard a movement. The neigh of another horse. Not the posse, please God, and not some heathen braves. And not some escaped convicts, either. A school marm, maybe, lost in her own dark fears.

Before I could move, before I could sit up, I saw black boots walk into the light of the fire. Saw them kick at the edge of the charred wood. Heard soft laughter. The figure stood, towering over me. The face, so distant, so far above the flame, was shrouded in the blanketing darkness.

My eyes worked their way up the body, trying to see.

Up the black boots of thick and filthy leather, their pointed toes wrapped in silver. Past the calves, the knees, the thighs that pushed hard against the tight-fitting denim. Past the crotch. Past that only with an effort. Past the silver belt buckle that glinted near the flame.

I continued working my eyes, hoping to pierce the night, to see the man who stood between me and my rifle. My eyes managed to make out that man's shirt, white with red piping, a shirt that seemed as if it were being pulled out from the trousers, opened button by button.

At first, I was sure that it was a trick of the dim, flickering light. But soon I saw the dark hair of his chest, in the shape of an American eagle, its head toward his muscled throat, its wing extending to each nipple, its tender slim tail weaving its way down the abdominal ridge and beyond.

My body, only moments before tense beyond measure with fear, relaxed and then began to tense again in a new way.

Slowly, I raised myself to my elbows, still resting on my back. Slowly the figure removed the shirt and threw it on the open fire. Sparks raised to the stars in heaven. The fire popped and hissed. The horses skimmed wild noises from their throats, and I saw my blacksmith's face in the churning firelight.

"You best be worth all the trouble it was finding you again," the hulking man said as he helped me to a kneeling position, holding me by the manly golden mane that rippled to my shoulders.

As he pulls me, he speaks, "What's yer name?"

"Wildroot," I gasp, and take one quick, deep breath as he yanks me to him.

Somewhere, a coyote is howling. . . .

1

You'd love Dr. Dutchman's office. I know you would. I've been in any number of therapist's suites, and I've never seen one I like better.

See, I sort of think of doctors' offices the way I do singles' bars. Some are too filled with ferns. Others have too much leather. Not Dina's — Dr. Dina Dutchman's — office. And it's not too doilied like Aunt Martha's living room, either. It's just a sunny place. Something that, at night, you could mistake for a performance artist's space. Good lighting, you know. When I'm sitting there talking to Dina, I feel like the amber spot takes years off my face.

Plus, when you talk to Dina, you get to sit across the round table from her, sipping herbal tea. It's like getting to sit at the adult table at Thanksgiving for the very first time. Acknowledgement of peerage, or something.

She's sitting across from me right now. She's wearing an olive-drab outfit, like always. Her legs are crossed, left over right, at the ankle. She asks me about the dream I've just related. "Do you often fantasize that you are a cowboy, Wyatt?"

"Wildroot, call me Wildroot," I say, leaning in a bit closer over the red zinger. "And, by the way," I ask, "why don't you wear a darker lipstick?"

"I'm not sure," she says, rolling her head around slowly to the left. She does this when I'm being cagey, when she's getting irritated. When I'm worse still, she does her yoga breathing and sounds like a radiator on the first cold day in November. When she rolls her head, her soft brown hair twirls slowly around also. She must use a free-holding mist. No spray. And yet, not a hair out of place. And too soft for mousse.

"I'm afraid that it might make me look too harsh," she said, finishing her thought.

"Not harsh. No, European," I correct her. Like Bianca Jagger. Like any number of folk before they enter the Betty Ford Institute. With mystery and flash. Like what they called Tallullah Bankhead's mouth — an angry jam jar. With lips like that, Dr. Dina Dutchman could speak with a whip for a tongue.

Like Lucy she is — that dumb little Lucy who gets all dotty over Dracula, even though Jonathan Harker can see through him in a moment. No, she just swings the window open and lets the bat in. But, change her lipstick and she could look like Lucy in the "After" photo — with the blood spreading down her lips.

Dina has noticed that my eyes went out of focus. She is sipping at her tea to hide the fact that she studies me from behind narrowed eyes. Her eyes are a soft, quiet blue that would awaken nicely with a little metallic blue shadow.

I mention this to her as she puts down her cup.

"Wyatt—"

"Wildroot."

"Wildroot, why do you try to remake me?"

She sets her cup down with triumph. With a soft wet thud.

"It was just a suggestion."

There is a long, long pause. Dr. Dina wants me to say something more. To reach some sort of insight. I set my jaw as if for the vice-principal.

The stand-off continues until Dina pours more tea into

her earthenware mug. Squeezes honey from the smiling plastic honeybear. No tea for me.

"Let us go back to the work we were doing discussing your mother," she concludes. I look at my watch. Half an hour left. Might as well. I discuss the dress that my mother wore one New Year's Eve when my father was stationed overseas. A dress that made her look like Auntie Mame. Which made her act like Auntie Mame.

As I speak, my eyes work the room. My mind goes other places. As if I split in two. One of me doing earnest work with Dr. Dutchman, my little Euro cookie, the other floating around the room like a helium balloon.

This is what we're working on, Dr. Dutchman and me, this floating feeling, this vagueness. This inability to act. It is, she is sure, brought on by my problem telling the difference between fact and fiction.

"I remember her cooking and cleaning, I guess," I am saying about my mother. "But mostly I remember her laughing. If she ever had time for anything, it was laughing. Sometimes, she'd fall from her chair at the dining-room table. Laughing so hard that the tears came and then dried and she was still laughing. Laughing made her look just like Judy Garland did when she cried.

While I'm relating this, I am seeing Dr. Dina Dutchman, dressed as an Amazon. With spear and hollow tube through which she blows poisoned darts. She wears a leopard skin that barely makes her decent. Like Raquel Welch in *One Million B.C.*

Tea being poured into my mug returns me to the office. She's trying to get my attention back. She's trying to finish off the pot.

Dina is looking at me with a bit of alarm. "Can't you pay attention enough to finish a sentence?" her eyes are asking.

Dina, Dina, don't worry so. Where I live is a pretty

place. And when it isn't, it's like the weather in Oklahoma; just give it a minute and it will change. Dina. Dina. In your cool linen suit. It's not even rumpled. Your accessories match your shoes and your bag.

I'm wearing underwear that has "Thursday" sewn onto it. Even though it's only Tuesday. I'm always racing too quickly. Using things up too fast.

A memory flicks into place. My mother has come home from the grocery store. It is Saturday morning and I'm wearing a striped tee shirt and loose jeans. I'm seven, maybe eight. I'm watching Bugs Bunny. Mother comes into the living room. Stands in front of the set to hand me a box of Little Debbie Devilsfood Cakes. My favorites. She puts the box down into my greedy lap and runs her hands through my hair. "Just remember, that's for the whole week," she says.

But Monday the box is empty, and although it makes a fine home for G.I. Joe, I want more cakes. I ask politely, then whine, conjole, and plead. Mother putters around the kitchen. Listening for a bit. Then her open palm fits over my mouth softly, quieting me. "I said, when it's gone, it's gone," she says sweetly. Irrevocably.

When it's gone, it's gone. There's a breakthrough for you. Me in my "Thursdays" on Tuesday. By Saturday, they'll all be gone, too. I open my eyes to Dr. Dutchman. To tell her what I've just experienced. Too late. She holds a blowpipe between clenched teeth. Pulls darts out of her leopard skin.

She's back to being an Amazon.

2

Now I tell all about myself.

I wear glasses. I have always worn glasses. I believe that, as a fetus, I floated about in my mother's belly with tiny little glasses on my face.

As a child, I was forced to wear those rectangular black framed glasses, the kind that only Woody Allen and/or Masons wear anymore. But then the late sixties came and I wore little round glasses on the end of my nose. Just like John Lennon. They were small enough that my range of vision extended to objects directly in front of my face and those up to two feet away to the left or right.

I then switched to wire-framed aviator glasses, which I wore for most of the seventies, except for a brief Spider-Creatures-from-Mars phase, which was an offshoot of the Lennon years. The Spider glasses were square, gray-tinted and large enough to cover the upper two-thirds of my face.

I now wear round horn-rimmed glasses. Plain brown things that, because they were created by a "designer," set me back many, many dollars. They are, without a doubt, my favorite glasses, as I am convinced that they enable me to fade into any cream or brown tinted background.

To be honest, I have many pairs of glasses now. They are a fixation for me, as I have just given up wearing contact lenses and have a prominent red horizontal vein running across one eye. My return to glasses has caused me to buy big ones, little ones, red ones — which are everywhere

these days — and clear-framed ones. I often carry more than
one pair with me, to change with my moods. If I could find
a way to wear more than one pair at once, I would.

My name is Wyatt Richard Wilde. My parents, no doubt,
thought that it sounded safe. And basically it is.

Names are another fixation with me. Juliet in no other
part of the play shows herself to be a fourteen-year-old idiot
kid as she did when she asked, "What's in a name?" In a
name is definition. Statement. And, most of all, perception.

It is this perception — the fact that others are deciding
their opinion of you just from the sound of the word that
identifies you — that is the basis of my obsessive behavior.
Or the "obsessive behavior" that Dr. Dutchman considers
it to be. But we made a deal, Dina and I. When dinosaurs
walked the earth. Five years ago when I started seeing her
twice a week on Tuesdays and Thursdays regular as
clockwork. We made a deal that I could try out any other
name I wanted and that she — Dina — would call me this
name until I changed it to another. She only made the deal
because she thought I'd try a name or two and then go home
to Wyatt. But, I ask you, if you were fitted with a glove like
Wyatt — a real slap-a-towel-at-him-in-gym-class moniker if
there ever was one — would you go back? So five years have
brought a potpourri of nomenclature. A melange of
phonetics. A cornucopia of Proper Nouns.

That which Dr. Dina "The Flying" Dutchman terms
"obsessive behavior."

I started seeing Dina about my Out-of-Body Experiences.
Times when I felt as if I were floating out of myself and off
to another place, another time. At first I sought help and
considered a disciple of Edgar Cayce, but decided first to

try the assumption that my trouble was psychological and not psychic in nature.

And I discovered Dina. Within our first year of working together, Dina unlocked the fact that my first Out-of-Body Experience took place while trapped in a locker during gym class. Several of my classmates found it to be extremely funny. I discovered the wonders of Nepal. Or at least of the Nepal that I had locked away in my brain.

We also figured out that I would have fewer Out-of-Body Experiences if I had more In-Body Experiences. It has been with this underlying theme that Dina and I have done most of our work.

Another motivation behind my continued work with Dina is my Traveling Pain. Now this term could be taken in several ways, I know, from unwanted relatives who come to visit, to an unhappy journey to Ohio. But my pain usually starts right between my eyes. From there, it's like Tinkerbell, flitting here, floating there, sometimes shining bright, sometimes growing dim. But there, ever there and present.

I have, at various times, been quite sure that I had a brain tumor, a broken wrist, vented spleen, and burst appendix. All were the many moods of the Traveling Pain.

My first visitation of Traveling Pain was this:

I was standing in one of those chain bookstores. In the classic section. I was hoping against hope that they would have someting a little more exciting than C. P. Snow. He was back in vogue then. This was years ago. D. H. Lawrence, maybe. Henry Miller. Herman Woulk they had — in classics yet. So I'm reading the spines of these books, my index finger tapping against my front teeth, and I notice this guy is staring at me out of the corner of his right eye. He's pretending to be reading the poetry section, but he's looking at me.

Now, I'm young at this time, twenty maybe, and home for summer vacation. Which means another hot time in West Virginia. So, I have no idea what to do about it. Hell, I don't

even know how I felt about it. So, I bend down to the W
through Z section, which proves to be just the right thing
to do, from this guy's point of view. He moves in closer. I
straighten up quickly and there's this jab of pain right
between my eyes. Not so much like a headache, as like
someone puncturing my skull with a red-hot letter opener.

I figured that I'd stood up too quickly and that the blood
was flowing upstream or something. I sort of staggered a
bit and then wandered off into the bed-and-bath shop next
door. I fingered a good many fitted sheets before wander-
ing back out into the mall. And there the guy was, leaning
next to the card kiosk. I walked down toward the record
store. He followed.

We stared at each other across the rock bins. He had
a shirtless Peter Frampton behind him and a little to the left.
Tight jeans and a college tee shirt. He was the kind of guy
who stood with his thumbs looped through his belt loops.
The kind who grins from ear to ear.

Now, this had been going on for a good twenty minutes.
Maybe half hour. And I'm staring at Barry Manilow albums,
actually considering buying one, because I don't know what
to do. Finally, he asks, "Do you want to go for a ride?"

And someone, I swear to God, takes the red-hot letter
opener and jams it into my lower back. I drop the Manilow
album. And I sort of dance back a step or two. Both the guy
and Peter Frampton look vaguely amused.

"Sure." I push my glasses back up my nose. They rest
right up against my eyebrows.

So, now I follow him. We don't talk, or even walk
together. I follow him out through J. C. Penney's and into
the back parking lot. It's late on a hot afternoon. Part of me
through this whole follow march is ready to back off and
run to my mother's Mustang, which is parked on the
opposite side of the mall.

We get to a yellow Cougar. He walks to his side and

unlocks it. Reaches over to unlock the passenger door. And the letter opener flies at my stomach, as if shot from a cannon. I see the tan of his skin up this arm and down the front of his shirt as he unlocks the car. I see a few hairs poking out of the top of his shirt.

I quickly get into the car. The black leatherette burns against me, hot from the sun. And another letter opener flies into my stomach.

At that moment, he asks, "You got an apartment?"

I open the glove compartment to cover my pain. Flip through insurance papers. Lean my head against the black leatherette dash. Finally, I turn my head toward him, still leaning and say, "No."

He looks a bit put out by this point. It occurs to me that although he seems twenty or so years older than I do in experience, this guy is maybe a year or two older in reality. And I begin to suspect that this is his mother's Cougar.

"We could just drive out into the country," he says.

Although I like his voice and would truly like to see what lurks under the jeans and tee shirt, another letter opener flies in. I close the glove compartment and put my head between my knees. All in one motion.

Leaning down again proves to be just the right thing to do, from his point of view. I feel a warm dry hand reach into the back of my pants. Another letter opener, a really big one that is really, really red-red-red-hot flies into my stomach, right into the navel. My head flies up at the exact moment that the glove compartment, which I'd poorly closed, drops open. The head and compartment door meet with a thud.

It's all a bit too much. To become the Saint Sebastian of the secretarial set. To have a hand on a part of my body that has received little attention to date. To slam my head into the glove compartment door. And I throw up on the floor of the college guy's mother's yellow Cougar.

He didn't even drive me around to my own car.

Which rather overtly brings us to another reason for my
work with Dina. H-O-M-O-you-know-what. Just the thought
of it causes my grandmother to light candles in front of
saints' statues. The idea of little Wyatt, who posed in front
of the Christmas tree in his sixth year of life with an army
helmet on, saluting like John-John Kennedy, the very idea
of his rolling around on the bed with another man, this
causes great familial grief.

Which causes — no, caused — no again — causes me
great familial guilt. That I should not give Granny any great
grannettes. That, worst of all, I should get arrested some-
day marching in one of "those" parades. Or in one of
"those" bars. Things that would force the family to move
to another country and start over.

It was never my own sexual preference (and I know
what you're thinking right now — he's been in therapy for
years and can't use the word "gay," right? Well, I can. Gay,
gay, gay. See?) that caused me guilt. It was, rather, other
people's preference.

From very early on, I can remember being much more
interested in what men could do than what women could
do. I remember once going into a gym with my father and
being rushed right out again after pointing at the existing
matter between all the men's legs.

To be honest, my parents never punished me for what
was, for me, a natural reaction to what I thought was a
wonderful invention of nature. They just stood by somewhat
bewildered and hoped that I would meet the right girl, who
would turn me around.

Which I did, for a while. And that was Pixie, who with
her parents and her brother Rollo, moved next door to my
family when I was fifteen.

Pixie and Rollo. As in any good story, the names have been changed to protect the innocent. Therefore, you should know that Pixie is not her real name.

And you should have figured out by now that Rollo is scum.

Pixie and I were quick and natural friends, as both our lives revolved around the mall that was located two miles from our doors. At fifteen, neither of us could drive. But, if worse came to worse, we were both fully prepared to walk the two miles if we had to. Most often, however, Rollo — who was seventeen and driving on his own — would take us.

Our summer days worked like this: Pixie and I would meet out under the grape arbor at about ten A.M., at which time Rollo was already busy cutting things down. That's what he did all summer — chopped and mowed. And when he finished mowing, he'd hack or chop. He'd start at about nine, wearing cut-offs and a tee shirt. By ten, he would have removed his shirt and was using it to mop off sweat. I had no idea that a seventeen-year-old could be so hairy, so I found it interesting to watch.

Which is what Pixie and I did with our mornings — watched Rollo mow. Sometimes, if we could take no more of his moving in concentric circles on the lawn, we'd go across the street to the shooting range and knock a bucket of golf balls down the gently sloping plane of the range. But mostly we watched Rollo sweat and breathed in the gas fumes of the mower. Around eleven, we'd start whining about the mall. Who was going to be there today. How good McDonald's would be for lunch. We'd just talk louder and louder until Rollo would stop the engine, sigh broadly, and say, "Come on."

He'd get the car keys off the hook in the kitchen and tell us to get in the car. He'd throw his shirt over his shoulder like a scarf and we'd drive off to the mall. As we walked in the door of the McDonald's, Rollo would pause in the doorway, blocking both the entry and the exit, to pull his shirt over his head. Right in front of the NO SHIRT, NO SHOES, NO SERVICE sign. It was activities like this that lead me to suspect that Rollo knew how good his body was. All that mowing had left him with shoulders like continental shelves. And, while watching him, it was always my particular joy to watch the muscles of his back ripple as he hauled the mower out of a gully.

All this fixation with Rollo might lead you to suspect that Pixie was not attractive. Or that, if she was, I never noticed. Not so. In fact, she was very pretty. With that odd combination of brown eyes and golden hair, where Rollo's hair had darkened into brown.

And it was Pixie who would become the first person with whom I was ever involved. And this, of course, happened out on the shooting range. It would have happened in the mall, but it was too crowded.

It was late on a June night. The kind of evening in which the day's heat stays with you. When everyone is out on their porch. As my family was. As was Pixie's. The two of us were sitting on the stone wall between our houses, she with her legs dangling on our property, me with mine on theirs.

We decided to go for a walk. She walked down her driveway looking at me. I walked down ours, looking over at her. At the end of the driveway, we turned left. And walked up over the hillside to a nearby farm.

It was one of those perfect nights. A half-moon lit the sky enough for an ambler to find his way. The cows and horses on the farm were making their contented animal noises. The mulberry trees were filled with fruit which we picked and ate as we walked along.

We looped the farm and came to the shooting range. The little shacks that, every twenty feet or so, held the golf balls and clubs, stood as solid shadows in the moonlight. Pixie and I joined hands to walk down the sloped lawn. We walked, then ran, then tumbled as the slope got steeper. We ended with arms, legs, hair and mouths intertwined at the base of the hill. I remember thinking that this was just like a Doris Day/Rock Hudson movie — not knowing until years later how very apt the allusion was.

If Pixie hadn't taken me in hand, it would have ended there. But she was on top of me in moments. Had us both relatively undressed seconds later, and climbed back on top.

What I remember best were her kisses. Soft and warm but demanding. As if her mouth had grown twice its normal size. And she shook her summer-short hair in my face and eyes, and then guided it down my body, the hair just barely brushing against bare skin. And then she bit my nipples, hard. By now, I was seeing only sparks of color and could hear only the ocean's roar.

Somehow, I completed the act of sex. Not by thinking of a man, but by not thinking at all.

After we'd finished, she stroked my lips once with her index finger and tossed me my clothes. By now she had my interest. I wanted to explore her body — the first nude woman's body I'd ever seen, albeit seen in the light of a half-moon. But we were dressed in seconds and running back up the hill.

A dog barked in the blue house as we ran by. His barking woke the collie in the yellow house next to the blue one. Both barked and woke a third and then a fourth. By the time we reached home, sweat-soaked and out of breath, every dog in the neighborhood was howling. The noise swelled like an audience applauding.

Just before the Fourth of July, I took a little evening walk with Rollo. I had recently spent a little more time talking

with him and had even helped a bit with the raking up of
the mowed grasses. His conversations tend to be a bit
monosyllabic, but his biceps went on for syllable after
syllable.

There was the smell of rain in the air. The night was
very dark. The farm animals, as we looped the low wooden
fence, spoke uneasily in grunts and whinnies.

At last we reached the shooting range. I could barely
make out the little huts against the overcast night, but I hit
Rollo lightly on the shoulder as I ran past and down the
hillside.

"You're it," I called out, for lack of a better come-on.
"Catch me."

Now, I wasn't really sure of what I was going to do next.
Whether it was better to be caught or not. So I just kept running. Soon I could hear panted breaths coming up behind
me. Fast. I began to run in serpentine. And then, BAM. For
in tripping over a root, over I went. I rolled a bit down the
hill before thudding to a halt. Rollo loomed over me. "You
okay?" he asked. I didn't answer. He leaned down closer.
I grasped him by the back of the neck.

If I hadn't taken him in hand, it would have ended there.
But I was on top of him in moments. Had us both relatively
undressed seconds later, and climbed back on top.

What I remember best was his hair. Fur, really, a pelt.
I remember running my chin against the hair on his chest
and arms, dangling my hands inside his thighs.

I shook my summer-short hair in his face and eyes and
then guided it down his body, the hair just barely brushing
against bare skin. And then I bit his nipples, hard. By now,
I was seeing only sparks of color and could hear only the
ocean's roar.

I looked at Rollo's face. From what I could make out,
he appeared to be stunned. He moved not a finger, neither
to put his clothes back on, nor to join me in my explorations.

And so, I continued on alone. A little like necrophilia, perhaps, but here was a warm, gorgeous man, and I wasn't going to waste him.

Much later, we put our clothes on slowly and trudged back up the hill and past the golf huts. We walked a bit in silence. Finally, Rollo said, "It's gonna rain any minute."

Both Rollo and Pixie treated me somewhat differently after that. At first, we confined our activities to walks — nature outings. Pixie and me and then Rollo and me, neither knowing about the other. I figured it should run along pretty smoothly, after all, there was no chance of ending up with double prom dates with these two.

It went pretty much the same way all summer. Pixie would take me to some new spot — in a tree or beside a lake, and then I would take her brother there to do to him what she'd done to me. Occasionally making the necessary changes of body build. Only once did Rollo refuse to play along: "No kissing!" he hissed and then turned his head away. And he never joined in actively, as if his lying or standing very still made him an innocent dupe. All in all, it wasn't a bad summer.

Now, you may wonder why I referred to Rollo as scum. The reason is very simple.

That fall, Rollo and Pixie enrolled in the same school that I was in. Pixie and I were in the tenth grade. Rollo was in the twelfth. As they'd moved in during the summer, they were new to the school.

Pixie and I continued on as we had before, best of friends. We rode together on the school bus, ate lunches together. Rollo, on the other hand, got in big with the varsity crowd. He got on most of the athletic teams. He changed. In the school hall, he swaggered when he walked. On the bus, he sat in back with the loudmouths while Pixie and I sat up front with the science and math types. When we got together in his room or mine, Rollo would just stare up at the ceiling with a pained expression while I twisted his nude body this way and that.

Now, it was this year also that I began to be locked in lockers and in general tormented by the varsity crowd. I guess I asked for it by hanging around the shower room a lot more than my schedule necessitated. I even considered becoming water boy.

Once the harassment began, it was to continue for months. Until attention spans wore out and another target was chosen. It became particularly difficult to ride the bus. In school, you could dodge and run. On the school bus, you could only pray that they'd turn on someone else.

One day they were being particularly mean. The usual words, faggot and fairy. They were taunting, threatening, and playing with their zippers. And I looked over at Rollo, who was, of course, sitting with them. Who could have stopped them by speaking up. Just by saying something like, "Come on, guys, this is boring."

Rollo looked at me. That same pained expression. Then he joined in with them, calling names and throwing things.

I never saw Rollo after that. Well, once more. It was after two years had passed. Rollo had gone to college that year, after working for a year in a local grocery store. I used to watch him bag other people's food while I bought for my family. Watch his biceps work.

And so he went off to college. And I became a senior, which is a fairly inevitable thing to be. Torment died down and things went smoothly. I had a crush on a boy named Thomas who was in my speech class. He had black hair and deep, dark eyes and wore fisherman knit sweaters. But I did nothing about it.

One night at the end of his first year in college, Rollo
came over to visit. Out of the clear blue sky. I had just
graduated and was preparing to go off to state college in the
fall. It seemed strange to see him again, bigger and stronger
than ever and stuffed into some tight blue jeans.

We went back to my bedroom. Rollo sat on the edge
of the bed. I sat on the floor in front of him. And we talked
a bit about college. He was in the R.O.T.C. and he told me
about that, about the drills and the other guys.

And we finally talked about sex. He told me that he had
finally had a woman while away at his first year of school.
"You ever had real sex?" he asked and seemed to be genuine-
ly interested.

"No." I lied.

Talked veered to other things. Unimportant things. Finally, Rollo said, "You'll really like college, Wyatt, you can do
whatever you want."

There was something in the way he told me to "do
whatever I wanted" that let me know what the real message
was.

"Yeah?" I said, and reached for his pants. That night
I drew blood and then I never saw him again.

With Pixie it was different. She figured out that the sex was
never going to be great between us and soon gave up on
it. And we became good friends. Actually, we still are, having both gone to state college and then moved on to the same
city. We still talk, usually about her lovers and my lack of
same. She knows my interests. But I have never told her about
Rollo.

Right now, I work as a display person in a big department
store. A chain store that you'd know by name. But I've done

other things — catered, run bookstores, worked in
restaurants. My mother just shrugs and calls me a late
bloomer. Says that I'll find my niche soon. I think she means
in more ways than work choices.

My father died a few years back. My mother lives on
her memories and hopes. I hope to take the postal service's
mail carriers test next fall and to earn some serious money.

When I'm at work in the department store, I work with
big themes. Not Thanksgiving or Easter, but life and death,
fear and hope, shadow and light. My displays are something
to see.

There. Now you know all about me.

3

Damn *Japs.*

*Four days ago it was. Four days ago. I'm standing out
on deck of the U.S.S.* Porcupine, *most feared battleship in
the Navy. On board is a group of the brawniest fightin'
marines that the midwest ever turned out. They're chewing their bullets, just waiting for the landing, so they can
slaughter the slant eyes and make the world safe for
democracy.*

*Four days ago, out of the noonday sun come the
airplanes. The Sacred Wind, they call them. Kamikazes;
pilots who don't expect to return alive, so they don't much
care about how they die, see. They just want to take you
with them.*

I was the first to see them come out of the clouds.

Yelled my head off warning the guys, but it was too late. The world exploded around us. We barely had a chance to return fire. There's smoke, there's screaming — the sound of those naturally deep, throaty voices gone falsetto in panic — there's pain. Metal flies and buries itself in my leg and pitches me overboard.

I'm swimming the best I can as I watch the ship pitch and roll, watch it go down. So much faster than I would have thought possible. No time for anyone to stand on deck and sing hymns.

I thrash my arms and work my legs as best I can. Something bumps against me, and then, within the wreckage and the panic, I see the top fin. Sharks. Damn sharks, I think, they're here to feed, brought here by the blood and death all around me. The blood pouring from my own leg is calling to this one like a hooker in a red dress on a hot summer night.

One lucky kick hits it on its tender nose. Buys me a minute. My last minute, I'm sure. I'm trying to get distance, swimming with my head down, when I hit into something soft ahead of me. A human arm touches me.

A corpse. I'm damned sure it's a corpse. The shock of it sends my head up for air. And I look into the two bluest eyes I've ever seen, as a doughboy pulls me onto the rubber life raft.

The doughboy is one of those Minnesota farm types. All muscle and no hair. He has torn away his shirt to bind my leg. Tells me that the bullets went right through and that the salt water helped clean the wound and that I should be just fine. He tells me this while he stares at me with those blue blue eyes.

I believe him.

One day out and we're thirsty and hungry. We swap life stories to pass the time, waiting for a ship to find us. No compass, no food, no oars, no sail — there's nothing else we can do but wait. He's Minnesota, all right. Named Johnny. But I keep on calling him Doughboy. At first he calls me Ensign Wildroot. Later, just Wildroot.

The second day, we're worse than hungry. Worse than thirsty. We're getting that haunted look that panic brings. When you're about to give up hope. We spend the day in silence, staring into each other's eyes.

The first night taught us that, no matter how hot the day is, the night is brutally cold. Doughboy is used to the farmland and the ocean unnerves him, especially at night. Each flying fish, each dolphin sends him jumping in fright.

I'm weakened from blood loss, colder that first night than I've ever been before. The second night, we know we have to pull closer if we are to survive. Doughboy takes what rags we're still wearing and makes them into a blanket. We lie together under the cloth for body warmth.

I can feel his breath on the back of my neck. Can feel the strong pulse of his blood flow. His strong leg curves between mine. I begin to relax my weight against his.

We begin to speak as if by accident. I hear a quiet sob break from his throat. Slowly, I roll over to face him. There is friction between our bodies. "I never been so scared," he says in his faint Norwegian accent. My hand raises to his smooth chest, moves softly back and forth between his nipples. They harden as his head rolls back into the night sky.

"We're gonna die right here, ain't we?"

His head comes to a rest on my shoulder. His heavy hand falls lightly on my abdomen. I lift his chin. "Listen," I say, "you saved my life by hauling me out of the drink. I would have been fish food by now. I'm gonna save you now, Doughboy, you just tell me how."

He never does tell me. Shows me, as his lips, already so close to mine, come down to rest so sweetly on my mouth. As his heavy body begins to cover and heat my own. . . .

The third day, we're ready to survive. Doughboy is grabbing at fish when I look out on the horizon to see our salvation. A small island. We paddle with our naked arms, shout with joy, and Doughboy carries me ashore to preserve my strength. My arms start by my sides, but slowly wind around his neck as we notice that no human rushes down to the beach to witness our arrival.

I rest under a palm tree, eating bananas as if they are steaks, while Doughboy scours the island. He comes back to say it's deserted. That night, we sleep out on the white beach, keeping each other warm.

Today, I'm walking slowly with the aid of a bamboo cane. I walk over the bluff just past the beach and watch Doughboy at work building our little hut. Just like a barn-raising on the farm, he says, but here his tools are rocks and his material is bamboo and leaves. He whistles happily while at work. As he turns and grins up at me from his labors, I see that he wears a palm leaf and an apron. As protection.

I slowly amble up to him, stand face to face, eye to eye. My hand slowly drifts from his bristle-short golden hair to his shoulder, his back, his hip, to the globes that he's left golden and exposed to the sun.

"Wildroot," he pants. "Oh, Wildroot."

Maybe the Japs ain't so bad after all. . . .

4

July 7
Dear Diary,

So, I'm working away on a new display concept. I've taken the entire store and transformed it into Dante's vision of Hell. I'm in women's shoes doing the circle of Hell that the liars go to. I've finished one dummy, she's the one standing in the rear. She has this red dress on and I frizzed her hair way out to here, and she bends from the waist, arms up and out like she just flung something. Her eyes blaze in the red light. Her mouth is vivid scarlet, twisted into a snarl. It's as if she's saying the worst thing she can think of.

In front of her stands another female dummy. Bolt upright. Coma-still. The victim of a remark. We are seeing the moment of impact, the moment before she can think to react in any way. She's just standing there helpless and totally vulnerable. One hand clutches her throat, covered only in a single strand of pearls. Her shoulders slump. Everything seems to sag. And yet, there is a subtext of strength about her. As if she, too, in other moments, has been the one standing behind, screaming the violent remarks.

It causes the viewer to ponder what each has done to be consigned to Hell. Why do they deserve punishment? "There are no innocents in Hell," the tableau seems to say. "Question your own innocence," it seems to demand.

And then, into the shopper's line of vision, into his or

her own consciousness, come shoes. Shoes shoes shoes. Mostly from Joan and David, my favorite designers. As if to say, "Here is innocence. Buy it."

So, here I am, busy at work creating his thing. Heloise is helping me. Her hair is blue this week, or looks so under the red lights. And I'm just arranging the cellophane under the foot of the dummy about whom the aspersions have been cast, when, looking up from her dainty plaster toe, I see this guy.

I've seen him in the store before. I wonder what he is doing in ladies shoes, but I soon see that he's just passing through. I tell Heloise that I need more cellophane, kicking the roll under the display table as I speak. And I walk off in pursuit of the guy, even though my office is the other way.

Now, this guy looks like I imagine Thor the Thunder God would if Thor were about 5'10" and slightly balding. Just very slightly. And his haircut, just on the verge of punk on the sides, covers the balding very nicely. Following behind, I see the perfect rear, the perfect waist. The shoulders are those of a meso-ectomorph. Average width, the kind that lead into naturally muscular arms, but the long slim muscles, like a tennis player, with little sweat bands around each wrist. And, thank God, the wrists are not too thin.

He's wearing green pants, the kind that come sans-a-belt. But I can change him after marriage. His white shirt reveals only his forearms, as the sleeves are rolled up to the elbow. Those forearms are thick and strong. Like he works with his hands.

He's a construction worker of some sort, I'm sure. But I picture him more as the kind that wears the hard hat and unrolls the design drawings and rides up and down on the little outdoor elevator, rather than the kind that sits and whistles at women during lunchtime. I picture him having his lunch in his little cabin on the worksite where he keeps all his designs. His job is to oversee, but the men look up to him, because he's not above swinging a hammer himself, and often pitches in when work is behind schedule. He's the kind that the guys buy beer for at Miller Time. Thor stops just outside the department store. He's reading a paper he just bought. He looks at something in the paper, then folds it under his right arm. He stands, waiting for something or someone. I wonder why he keeps looking at his hands.

I'm standing in front of Thor now, looking at him over the paper I bought right after him. I can't see much of his chest, as his shirt is unbuttoned only at the top button. He's wearing a green and brown tie, slightly loosened at the neck. His Adam's Apple is a bit pronounced. I hope for a deep, rich voice. I picture the two of us on the beach at Acapulco, slick with oil.

I must have been staring, because he looked up and our eyes met for a moment. He has faded blue eyes, like denims get after many a wash. His eyes look wise and look as if they might deepen in color in moments of passion.

I'm afraid I sighed when I looked at him. He looked again at his hands and then cleared his throat.

I try to think of what to say. I am still thinking of what to say when he walks over to the glass elevator and gets in. I watch him ascend. He is wearing brown loafers. But I can change those, too, after we're married.

5

I only have to mention Thor briefly and in passing to hear Dina use the word "obsessive."

There is no talking to her when she gets like this.

It's just that she had been playing Wagner when I came in, which enhanced my notion of her as a Valkyrie, plucking the brave dead off to Valhalla, and the Thor story just came out. Her brows furrowed immediately, which caused me to shorten my tale. But not short enough. She didn't even make me any tea.

"Why can't you ever allow the objects of your fantasies to be just ordinary men?" she asks me, or something to that effect.

I try to explain that it excites me to think of men who interest me as being larger than life.

"Unobtainable, you mean," she counters. "This is part of the root system of your problem.... Wildroot." There is always that little pause before she can bring herself to use that name. "You place people — men, specifically — above the range of humanity and then you allow yourself to feel inferior to them. You can then permit yourself to remain withdrawn. Fantasy-wracked."

This doesn't sit well with me. I do not consider myself to be wracked by my fantasies. And I say so.

She is about to sigh broadly. I know that she is about to sigh.

Dina looks at her telephone for a moment, as if willing

it to ring. She shakes her head ever so slightly from side to side. She sighs broadly.

I fold my arms across my chest and stare at the Boston fern. We are silent for a very long time.

Finally, Dina makes tea. Orange spice. Caffeine-free.

Before long we're talking again. I try to explain that it is hard to talk to her sometimes. That she can be very judgmental. She insists that she is merely trying to help me see the big picture. Her big picture, I reply. She pours the tea too quickly and smoking liquid floods her desk. I can see that she is angry and that makes me angry. You can't tell some therapists anything. I suggest that we talk about some of my recent dreams, thinking that I can make something up to please her. She, blotting the spilled tea off her desk, insists on more information on Thor.

Before I know what I've done, I admit to having followed him three times this week. I hang my head with shame. She walks around to the front of her desk, lifts my chin with her smooth hand. "It's not your being interested in this Thor that I object to," she says, and I know that this is only because the AMA no longer lists homosexuality as a disease. "It is your inability to confront the situation head-on. It is the following, the skulking, that is inappropriate behavior."

How many times have I heard that before? "Inappropriate behavior." There's Dina the Valkyrie, passing the dying Goths and Visigoths by, calling to them from her winged horse, "No Valhalla for you. Not with your inappropriate behavior."

Silence descends again, and remains for a good long time, and I pretty much find myself thinking that the session is just going to continue on like this, when I find myself saying that I am feeling that my life pretty much adds up to "sprawling insignificance."

Dina latches onto this like a five-year-old onto a honey graham cracker.

Before I know it, I'm on the couch. And I hate being on the couch. Not only because it's off-white, making me worry about stains of any sort, and not only because it's that burlappy kind of material that can scratch at you right through your pants, but also because lying prone in your doctor's office makes you feel like you're really giving in to therapy — like you just might really need it. It has a certain drowning feeling attached.

"Tell me about your first memory. The very first thing you can remember." Dina is sitting next to me in a leatherette sling-back chair. She is wearing a flowing olive-drab skirt with a tan blouse. The whole world seems to be neutral tones.

The question is a hard one, I say, winding my arms about me. Dina gives me her "there, there" look. I think a long moment, while staring at the begonia plant on the window sill. And then I remember:

"I'm sitting on one of those wrought iron chairs in someone's back yard. I must be very young because my feet don't even come to the edge of the chair. I can see my little shoes sticking out in front of the chair. It's dark green. I'm reaching up to hold my mother's index finger when we walk together.

"Holding the arms from below, I can see where the chair paint has flaked. Where, beneath the green, there is yellow and black and white. And I'm picking away at the paint with my little fingers. It's that same paint that was on all that old furniture. It doesn't break off, it bends back and peels.

"It must be early in the morning when I'm sitting there, because the chair isn't hot in the sunlight. And I don't remember being at all bored. I'm very content. Almost like a product on a shelf.

"And I can remember what must be the same day. And I'm walking. Or sort of floating. Some adult is holding my hands and lifting me just slightly, so that I can walk along those bricks that were turned at 45° angles to outline both sides of a sidewalk. The bricks stick up below like stalagmites, and my toes are just barely able to touch them as I swing by. I can remember finding that the funniest thing, that effortless floating.

"Or being carried out of the car when you fell asleep on the way home from visiting relatives. Every Sunday, we visited my mother's sister and her family. And every Sunday, on the way home from my aunt's house, I'd fall asleep in the car, turning into dead weight against my mother's chest.

"I can remember waking up after the car engine was turned off and after we'd gotten out of the car. But waking just for a moment. Just for a moment, as my father came around and took me from my mother's arms and then carried me into the house and up the stairs. My mother would have moved on ahead to get out my pajamas and turn down my bed. No noise awakened me again after I drifted back to sleep against the rough shoulder of my father's coat. But in that moment of wakefulness, I would have heard them shush each other, or laugh maybe.

"And maybe there's a brief memory in there somewhere of having my foot being jammed into my pajama bottoms, but, in the morning, I was always amazed by the magic of awakening in my own bed and my own pajamas, with the last thing I remembered being my aunt kissing me goodnight. . . .

"No one's carried me that way in years. . . ."

I'm still staring at the begonia. By now, of course. I'm crying.

6

I went to college for the same reason that millions of others do: to find a husband. It was after the Rollo experience — having the rare opportunity to compare and contrast Rollo with Pixie — that I was sure I wanted to involve myself with men. And this notion was reasserted upon me every time I found myself in the shower room in the dorm.

Suffice it to say I was the cleanest of undergrads, for our dorm had that gang shower room that has since become popular in prison movies and unpopular in schools.

But there's something so wonderful about the sight of wet and soapy men. How they all bend their heads back under the jet of the water. How they take so long to soap their underarms. The thicker and fuller the shoulders and arms, the longer it takes them to soap. And how they flip back and forth under the spray like pancakes on a griddle, ass to cock, cock to ass.

There's the firmness, to be sure, and the muscle, and the hairiness and the white teeth that seem to smile out all through the showering, but it's the unihibited joy that most loudly resounds in the men's shower room. There's something in a man — particularly in a college-age man — that revels in hot water. Like he revels in showing the power between his legs.

It wasn't until college that I managed the trick of taking in the body of the man across from me without his knowledge. Although my joy of the vision brought about many a Traveling Pain. In the head or in the stomach. But as much as they incapacitated my activities, they only increased the pleasure of my secret stares.

There were bodies with nipples like coffee-cup saucers, hugh and round and deeply colored. And there were pinprick nipples, that, when paired with a smooth chest, gave the man a Ken doll look. And there were chests and stomachs with wild fans of hair, and those with a few wavy strands. Navels were in and out, and below were the privates, some chestnut tiny, others swinging under their own weight as their owners lifted arms and head to wash.

I will not deny that I often wished that my hand could be the one soaping the balls — whether they hung loose or held themselves in tight — or lathering in the tight crack of the ass. This is, by now, obvious. But I will insist now because it is true, that the vision of these men, with their yellow hair narrowing down their bodies into a coarse brown fan, with their strong sculptured legs and their clear blue eyes, with their skin not yet stretched, yet filled rather, to its upmost limit with blood and muscle, I will insist that my fascination with these figures went well beyond the carnal. It was a world of unknown rites and enterprises, of surmounting strength and secret languages.

And it had my full attention.

This attention soon narrowed down and centered in on one man. Orly Kasaba. Never before had I seen skin of this color. Light caramel and glossy in sun or shade. And dark curling hair and eyes that should have been brown but were blue blue blue instead. Some said that his mother was a French actress and his father an African chief. I thought he looked just like Nicky Arnstein in *Funny Girl*.

Because of Orly Kasaba, I nearly majored in economics. Because of him, I became mascot to the football team.

Let me backtrack.

I met, or noticed, rather, Orly Kasaba on my second day on campus. It was a sort of mixer. The kind where everyone eats watermelon and then there's a tug-o'-war across a drying creek bottom that resembles a tar pit. Upperclassmen against freshmen. I was about the third freshman back from the front of the tugging line. The freshmen lost, naturally, and in we went into the pit. I was close enough to the front of the line to land on few and be landed on by many. Like a scene in *The Good Earth*. I was trying to make my way out of the mud when this tanned hand reached down from the bank. Naturally, it was Orly Kasaba, leader of the pack of the football team, who reached down like something off the Sistine ceiling to get the skinny guy out of the mud. Luckily, muddy as I was, it was hard for him to see my face or hair color, as I was all-over the shade of a clay pot.

I remember the look on his face. Like he expected the sun to glint off of his shining teeth, like he was about to call me "old sport."

I didn't even pay much attention to the other guys that day as we showered off the mud. Instead, I asked coy questions about Orly Kasaba. As I previously mentioned, some told me that he was the son of an African chieftan. Others that he was the only child of the Egyptian ambassador to the United Nations. Also that his mother was an actress, a poet, a scientist, and a sex expert. Clearly, there was much interest in Orly Kasaba and little hard information available. Only that his major was economics.

I, therefore, became interested in money. I took statistics to sit behind him and gaze at the back of his neck, at the spread of his hips. I enrolled in Econ 1023, having fudged my way past the required 1013 with tales of summer employment in offices of high finance. Here I sat to Orly Kasaba's right, and could take secret delight in his Adam's apple as it bobbled every time he swallowed.

That went on a good long while, and my grade point average plummeted, before I ran back to the school of design, where I belonged. But only after I hit on a new way of being near the boy I craved.

I had throughout the autumn taken to going to football games. Although I was never quite sure of just what was going on, I had figured out that Orly Kasaba was number 25, and that left me with enough to go on. I watched him run up and down the field in his tight little pants. Occasionally, I also watched the cheerleaders who leapt up and down between our team and its audience. Among the girls in their tiny little skirts was the figure of a huge black and red velour panther. Our mascot. Its job seemed to be to stroll among the cheerleaders and clap its hands and wave its arms. It occurred to me that these were the luckiest people. They stood on the field with the players, while I sat acres away trying to decide whether that was a 25 or a 22.

Now, at this point, I must mention that ours was a violent football team — even a brutal one. It comes with being raised in Middle America. It also comes with having a name like the Black Panthers during the early seventies. Our team members, in their red and black jerseys, slammed into anything that moved within their line of vision. And, thus, fate took a hand. For, one day, as I sat high above our forty yard line, the Panther mascot moved within their line of vision and was dragged several yards before anyone figured out that this giant stuffed animal of a thing was not on the opposing team. The Panther was carried off the field to tumultuous applause. I ran to the lockers, seizing the moment's opportunity. With great waving of hands and stamping of feet, I persuaded the coach to let me take the Panther's place, until the original could recover. Finally, he agreed. We slipped the sweaty man out of the pelt and into his jockey shorts. I fastened the suit around me.

I ran back onto the field.

The reaction was amazing. Pom-poms shook everywhere. The fans lept to their feet as they saw what they believed to be the resurrection of the Panther. I waved my arms and clapped my paws a little and went over to the stand by the cheerleaders. I then turned and stood leering within ten feet of the crouching figure of old number 25.

What can I say here that hasn't been said before about the power and glory of anonymity? In a black-and-red velour suit, you can do many things that you can't do in your own blue jeans. I found, for instance, that I could do splits of a sort and tumbles that left me, if not on my feet exactly, then at least unharmed. I found that I could lunge at the cheerleaders and that the audience would laugh. And that the cheerleaders would shriek and run from a giant velour cat just as they did from Harpo Marx. I also found that, if a giant cat is chasing cheerleaders, eyes turn away from the game and toward the action on the sidelines.

I thought that this was just great. I thought of myself as the permanent Panther, ripping my cat head off at the end of each game just for that brief moment of acclamation before Orly Kasaba and his teammates whisked me up and onto their shoulders to carry me home in victory. I saw myself as Orly Kasaba's personal mascot, I guess. And I thought that he would see me in the same way.

But I guess I should have noticed the look on 25's face, and on the faces behind the blonde number who'd tossed her pom-poms long before in sheer terror.

What can I tell you, I was naive. My worst crime, I guess, was reveling during a losing game. The black-and-red team was being slaughtered by the guys in orange and blue. Just before the final gun, the coach had his fill. "Knock it off," he screamed at me, along with some well-chosen obscenities. He stepped between me and my cheerleader and stuck his reddened face close to my black velour ears. He shoved me to the ground.

And so, instead of becoming the regular Panther, I was a picture in the next day's newspaper. The coach standing over the shoved mascot. I followed the team off the field at a safe and respectful distance. The cheerleaders stomped off together asking each other, "Who's the creep in the cat suit?"

But I hadn't counted on one thing in my depression — the locker room.

When the cheerleaders walked off the field, they turned left into the women's locker room. And I turned right into the roomful of men. I went over to the bench in the corner, on which lay my clothes. I began to take off the panther suit, reaching behind for the long zipper. I pulled it off my body, leaving the head for last. When I realized with relief that no one seemed to recognize me, or even care who I was, I relaxed and began to enjoy the scenery.

I followed the team into the showers. He was in there already.

Nude, in the shower, Orly Kasaba was hairy enough to look as if he were wearing some clothing of a different sort.

Among the bent necks of the defeated team, only his own lifted magnificently against the drilling water. Only he grinned against the black defeat. And his mouth grinned only because it was its natural position.

I took my good look and thought my nasty thoughts. Was this all worth it, or what?

As we left the shower room and dressed, a few of the soldiers grunted their displeasure at me. Orly Kasaba looked over at me just once, as he ran the towel between his legs. His look contained some vague recognition, but his eyes then went elsewhere. He didn't say a word to me. Not on that day or any other. My embarrassment was such that I was able to drop my load of economics courses and return to my own studies. And that I was able to spend my Saturdays doing things more to my liking than watching football.

But, on that fall afternoon, the irony of ironies was still to come. I was walking out the door of the locker room and heading down the hall. "You!" the coach bellowed. I took two more steps and he blew his whistle. "I said YOU!" he said. I stopped and he strode over to me, and rammed his face close to mine. "You go chasing girls on your own time, not while my men are fighting for their lives — understand?"

I said I understood. "Jerkoff," he continued. "You coulda been the Panther. But you had to blow the whole bit by chasing skirts."

It wasn't until much later — when I'd stopped shaking — that the ramifications hit me. That I'd lost the whole season in the showers with Orly Kasaba. But at that very moment, I was hit with the irony of ironies — I had just gotten kicked out because the coach thought I was chasing girls.

7

August 14
Dear Diary,

You have to thank God for a mall, don't you?

So much under one roof. It's hotter than hell outside, but in here, under the dome, it's perfect termperature and always daylight.

Now, this is the sort of insight that is not common for me to have — everybody knows that. I'm not one to sit and ponder the cultural import of a shopping mall. Not even one like this, with glassed-in elevators that ascend silently into the upper reaches of the restaurant level.

But I was in that elevator just today. My best friend Benny Roshomon was with me. We decided to go to this Mexican joint after work and get some frozen margaritas, since it was Tuesday and very hot outside and Tuesdays are Margaritaville days at this place, which is part of a chain of restaurants in the mock-adobe shape of a Mexican village, and the margaritas come in a glass the size of a goldfish bowl for just three dollars.

So Benny and I are sitting in the bar part of the restaurant, and it's shaped like a cantina of Old Mexico. And the waiter comes over and asks us if we want mild or hot sauce with our tortilla chips and Benny says, "Both." And, well, if it hadn't been so hot outside and if I had air conditioning in either my car or apartment, which I don't, I would have left right then and there. Because I know that he

answered "Both" just to upset the waiter, who looked at
the two of us like they looked at Oliver Twist when he said
he wanted, "More." Like we were missing the whole concept. That we were supposed to choose between the hot
and the mild hot sauces and not ask for both. Like this was
one of life's little choices and we were demanding too much
from life. Like he would have to go back to the kitchen to
get more crocks of hot sauces sooner than he wanted to.

Now, I have to explain a few things right here:

— First, it had not been the easiest of days. But it started
off just great. I decided to have the new displays throughout
the women's section be a tribute to the Gabors. Everything
Hungarian to celebrate the bold new colors of the fall line.
Everything looking like Lithuanian Easter Egg dye. So
everything Hungarian, right? That means goulash and the
Gabor sisters. So I tell Heloise, my assistant. First I tell her
to make the words BOLD NEW COLORS in big huge letters
and then I tell her to write out the names of the Gabors over
and over again to use along with the big blonde dummies,
no pun intended.

But I can't remember the sisters' mother's name, Mom-
ma Gabor won't cut it. So I wonder off around the mall,
leaving Heloise to work on the other three names while I
think of their mother's name.

It truly took me thirty minutes to think of Jolie Gabor,
and I'm proud of myself when I do, but, truthfully, I've
another reason to go for a walk. I'm hoping to see that
blond guy again. Thor. I've only just seen him once
since that first time (see July 7) and then there was just
that one brief second in the rooftop parking garage
when I saw him getting into his car (see July 23). I have
decided now that it was definitely a BMW and that I

was a fool for not writing down the tag number when I had the chance.

But Thor's nowhere to be seen. I've kind of come to the conclusion that he works here at the mall. Maybe somewhere in the bowels of the professional/medical level. So I go back into the store and there is Heloise. She is wearing too much makeup. Before I can tell her it's Jolie, I notice that she's hanging the Gabor names right now behind a dummy that's wearing a Halston glitz number in gold lame. And she has spelled Zsa Zsa as ZaZa and hung it all over the store. Instead of old Hungary, I get *La Cage*. It's just more than I can bear. Sometimes, I think that Heloise is a secret crack addict. That she runs into the washroom and melts it into a spoon, or whatever you do with it. Who the hell can't spell Zsa Zsa? So we have to take the signs down and scrap them. Start all over. But the damage has been done — dozens of women who ordinarily look to my displays for insight and inspiration think that I can't spell the name of Zsa Zsa Gabor. Me — who has seen *Moulin Rouge* more times than I care to remember.

But it gets worse.

— Second, I go to lunch in the department store lunchroom. I can't face the prospect of seeing any women carrying any shopping bags from our store in a restaurant. I'm sure that they'll be whispering from rouged lips to powdered face, "Can you believe that he can't spell Zsa Zsa?"

I'm still mad about it, as I bend over my hot chicken pot pie. I still can't believe that Heloise, when confronted, went all slack jawed and said, "Are you sure?" with a suspicious tone in her voice, as if I were possibly not sure. I directed her to check with the *Filmgoer's Companion* over at B. Dalton's over her lunch hour if she doubted me. Then I came in for my chicken pot pie. I've hated them since I was a child and decided that the chicken and vegetables —

peas, mostly, which I've never really liked — were held together by hot phlegm. The thought of it ruins you for chicken pot pies.

So I'm sitting and moving parts of the pie around on my cafeteria plate — I order them to punish myself when I fear that I've overreacted — when Mary Willowby sits next to me.

Now, I've always liked her. Or, rather, I've always liked her name quite well enough to put up with her nonsense. She is the head of giftwrap. The one who gave Benny Roshomon a job when I asked her to.

So she sits down next to me. She's having the taco salad. And she says, "I have something to say to you about your friend." She means Benny Roshomon. "You've got to talk to your friend about his corners," she says. "I don't mind that he's always at least fifteen minutes late or that he wears those sneakers that are held together by electrical tape. He says that the customers never see his feet and I guess that he's right about that. And I don't even really mind that his wrapping technique is a bit bizarre. Matching colors oddly and using the seasonal decorations out of their seasons. Although I know I'll regret his fondness for the reindeer when Christmas is coming and I can't get any more in stock because he's using them to wrap sunglasses and jams. But he simply has to see reason on the corners of the packages. I've shown him twice how to do it — tape the flap down, roll the paper over, trim and taper the ends, fold over and under, and tightly tape. It gives the corner a look that a marine sergeant would appreciate. But Benny's come out lumpy, like he was rolling tobacco in them. And he refuses to try to get better. I've had complaints about his packages. And today, I saw a customer helping him with a package. I don't know how much longer I'm going to be able to keep Benny on."

Now, news like this was the last thing I needed. And

it placed me at a crossroads. I should have spoken to her supervisor. Told her about Heloise's misspelling. But something in Mary Willowby's demeanor — her long suffering, perhaps — made me act like Vida in *Mildred Pierce.* I did everything but slap her in the face and steal her husband.

So I started to feel guilty and stopped by gift wrap on my way back to display. And I invited Benny to Margaritaville so that I could counsel him on corners. And I'm just about to mention them to him when I look up and see blond receding hair in the distance.

Thor is in the restaurant with another man. A man with brown hair and kind of a baby face. But with a heavy beard. A man with wide, large, dark eyes. A man who wears a turtleneck in the summer. A man like Rex Reed. At first I'm pleased. Perhaps this means that Thor indeed is the kind of man that Rock Hudson would have referred to under raised eyebrows as "musical." Then I'm very, very upset. If he is musical, then he is probably sitting with his instrument.

I kick Benny under the table. We lean in close. I tell him who is in the restaurant with us. He hurries to the bathroom in order to pass closely by Thor's table for a closer look. Coming back, he says, "He doesn't look like Thor to me. I think he's a gimp."

We're looking over at their table and the two men rise.

Benny feigns dropping his napkin and drops under the table, afraid that we've tipped our hand. But the two men just walk by, without speaking to each other. We pull money out of our wallets and hurry after the men, keeping our voices and eyes down as we follow them to the rooftop parking lot.

The smells of oil and gasoline rise into the hot, just-darkening sky. The two men amble toward the blue BMW. Benny and I split up to follow, just like they used to do on *Mod Squad.* Thor pauses to remove his sports jacket, a light cotton/poly blend in a rather severe plaid, before he gets into the car.

I'm standing two cars back and slightly to the left. I memorize the tag number — ZSA 147. And I look down at my shoes, laughing a little at the Hungarian irony of it all. When I look back up into the rear of the car, I see clearly that the two men are kissing.

8

There is the sound of trumpets in the air. In the cold, clear air of a Colorado autumn.

I am walking along a main street in Denver, wearing a tailored Armani suit, eel skin belt, and simple Oxfords. My silk tie is carefully knotted and dimpled. My briefcase matches my belt. My hair is cut quietly, but not solemnly. There is a trace of the punk. I am wearing Perry Ellis cologne. I smell like a young god.

I walk with a stride that is bold and yet staccato. Half march. Half dance step. I arrive in front of a skyscraper of an office building. The building's name is embossed upon its facade: Denver Carrington.

Inside, I ride the whisper-quiet elevator. Arrive upon a floor high above the streets below. A young man walks toward me, his hand outstretched to shake. His mouth is stretched into a friendly grin. The fluorescent light plays against his teeth, his dirty blond hair. Our palms embrace.

"Hello," he says as I look from his dirty yellow crown to his beautifully sad eyes, his broad shoulders, his

conservative suit, his Valentino silk tie, his simple black Oxfords. "I am Stephen Carrington."

I let go of his hand and follow him through a maze of secretaries at their desks. They type on silent keyboards. Everything is whisper-quiet.

From behind a door nearby, a woman shouts, "I'll get you for this, Blake. I'll make you very sorry for this." She has a clipped British accent. A moment later, she bursts through the doorway, a doorway through which her shoulders barely fit. She ignores everyone around her. She stands by the elevator and lights a thin cigar and waits for it to arrive.

I have looked away from my host for moments. And when I turn back, our eyes meet. "That was my mother," he says simply. And there is some discomfort within him. A greater, deeper pain within his eyes. As if he were a gentle man, lovingly caught between two parents, who are themselves locked in an eternal business rivalry, based in a lifelong passion of love/hate.

I follow my host into his office. Notice the honest and straightforward way he has of walking. Notice the strength of his muscular buttocks inside his perfectly tailored European suit.

Within moments, it seems as if our multi-million-dollar oil deal has been struck. There is to be a marriage of sorts between our multinational corporations. Each company depending upon the other. We look across the desk at each other as peers.

"It will take my secretary some time to put these papers in order for our signatures," he says. "Perhaps you'd care to have some dinner with me while we wait?"

I look across the desk at this man. Although he sits in a power position, with fingertips just touching, leaning back slightly in his chair, and although he has neither used the word "fabulous" in conversation, nor rolled his eyes toward heaven in my brief acquaintance with him, perhaps there is reason to hope.

I agree to dine.

As we are leaving the office, an older man approaches us. He is distinguished gray, a man of power. Stephen introduces him to me as his father. And tells his father that we are going out to dine. As the older man shakes my hand, I catch a moment's hatred in his eyes. And believe that I hear him utter one quiet word. I believe that word to be "DeNard."

As we leave the building, I am amazed that, in the seemingly brief moments that we were inside conducting business, it has grown dark outside. And soon we are looking across into one another's eyes over candlelight. Over the table of a fabulous restaurant. My eyes roll briefly to heaven.

There are moments while we dine in which our eyes meet, as if they were drawn into each other. In those moments, I feel as if there is a sharp intake of breath in him. It is as if I can also feel his heart pound.

We skip dessert.

We drive fast in his sports car. Drive wildly through the autumn night. The car's top is down. The heater blasts hot hot air. Wind whips through his hair as he stares straight ahead, driving faster, faster.

He stops finally at the edge of a high cliff. Around us is a pine forest. Below us is a drilling site. Oil derricks burst erect from the ground below. He turns and slowly faces me. His eyes say, "All this is mine." Within him is the gray-haired man, a man of ownership and power. But within him also is a boy, whose mind is wracked with pain.

His strong fingers slowly move up his chest. Slowly, slowly he opens his silk tie. Unbuttons one and then two buttons on his shirt.

I look from his fingers and their work into his eyes and

*then back to his hands as they fall into his lap. There is
a long minute of uncertainty. I wait for a cue, a sign.
Finally, I let my own fingers slowly knit with his, Then,
slowly, my fingers brush away, to caress his hand and the
thigh upon which it rests. My hands sculpt him then, move
more and more strongly — his thighs, hips, waist, chest.
The opened buttons, his muscular throat.*

*"Wildroot," he says, calling my name softly.
I lean myself toward him. Lips approach lips. His eyes
narrow with passion, and then open with alarm. His body
stiffens as I begin to open his belt.*

*"I can't!" he cries, "I mustn't" and he pulls away
sharply, turns his head away.*

*When again he turns in my direction, I can see the
tears in his eyes. He pulls me close, slowly, embraces me.
I feel his face against my own. He breathes in my Perry
Ellis and then his hands slowly turn my mouth to his.
And he kisses me then, slowly, slowly, and then deeper.
I feel his breath, his lips, the stubble of his beard. His
tongue.*

And then sharply he once again pulls away.

"No!" he bellows and runs from the car.

*My lean athletic body catches him with ease. He is
wracked with sobs, unable to see clearly. I encircle him in
my arms and we walk together in the night.*

*We walk to a campsite of his childhood with cabins
and forts. With tennis courts and a football field. I stop
us both on the archery field. I stand him in front of a straw
target. "Strip!" I command as I back away.*

*As I lift the heavy bow, I see his skin begin to gleam
in the moonlight. I see the muscular arms, the smooth chest.
The beauty of his sexual organs as they swing between his
massive legs. I understand his hesitation and his pain. The
decisions that he must and yet cannot make. His suffering
and the suffering he has caused. His goodness and his*

weakness. The kindness of his heart and his selfishness. His fears and his animal nature.

He stands nude, ten feet in front of me. As I lift the bow and arrow erect, he lifts his weapon also, the head of it glaring red even in the dim light.

I let the first arrow fly and catch him through the thigh upon which our hands have rested.

There is blood, there is pain, to be sure, but upon his lips is a beautiful smile. An aura of light encircles his brow. He stands with the wounded leg bent slightly before him.

I loose a second arrow, a third arrow, a fourth. And more still. I let them fly, piercing his shoulder, his waist, his neck, his groin. Blood pours from every wound. He lets loose a sigh of ecstasy.

My quiver is nearly empty. I let fly the last arrow. It pierces through his heart. His strong neck flies back, his dirty blond halo soars upward as an orgasm swells his organ, wracks his body. His eyes dance up to heaven.

"Fabulous!" he cries, and then he is no more. . . .

9

Movember 1

Dear Diary,

Three months now since I've put pen to paper. Three months now I've been off my feed.

That night in the parking garage, I ran off down the ramp. Benny followed and caught up with me in the park, where we sat for a long time and stared at our shoes.

Mine were beautiful woven brown leather. I finally told him
what I'd seen.

Benny was somewhat less than upset.

"So he has a boyfriend," he said. "So very big deal."
We had three scoops of gelati each and then went to
our respective homes.

A great deal has happened since then, dear diary.

First, Heloise quit one day, informing me that she was
in need of "Island Magic." She sent me a postcard from
somewhere in the South Seas. It amazes me that these
people may not have electricity, but they have full-color
postcards. I remember feeling slightly numb when she decided to go. I was doing back-to-school displays. And I think
that my decision to do back-to-school was what decided
things for Heloise. For weeks before she left, she took to
looking at me strangely, then to asking me what was wrong,
then to saying out loud things like, "I don't know, but you
used to be so cosmic in your display scope." So suddenly
nothing I could do with a mannequin made any sense to
me anymore. So suddenly we went to themes like fun-in-
the-sun and back-to-school. And what's wrong with
them? — crowd pleasers both.

True, last year we did a great Labor Day. With real labor.
Mannequins with pillows over their plaster stomachs. And,
true, suddenly the bottom fell out of my advertising
rationale. And truest of all, as I could feel Heloise slipping
away, it was the good news/bad news aspect of the situation that was getting to me. Good news: Thor was obviously available. I mean, there he was in the car with that other
guy. Bad news: Thor was not at all available, at least not to
me. I mean, there he was in the car with that other guy.

I don't think that I've felt this alienated and lonely since
they started publishing *Playgirl*, giving me full-color
naked friends to play with.

All of this has led to a crisis with Benny in these last

few weeks. In that he wanted Heloise's job. In that he acted like a pushy bastard and stopped at nothing to try and get it. In that I knew better, since he was hanging by a thread in gift wrap and saw this as an easy out. In that he thought that I'd never fire him, no matter how bad he was at his work or how late he came to work or how often he disappeared from his work station during the course of the day.

Instead, I hired a manchild named Byron. Manchild, affected as the word is — and it does sound like something that George Saunders would have called Hurd Hatfield — is the word that describes Byron. Short, very blond, and bewildered. Too old for being a boy, but still within the age range that gets away with almost anything by smiling. He came to me with no training. And he no doubt considered decoration to be the construction of paper chains before he came to work for me. Now he walks around with a measuring tape around his neck just like Heloise used to. Now he wears a can of mousse in his hair, which cascades perilously down over one eye. He has somehow also learned Heloise's old trick of tucking one's chin down and looking up at one's boss from lowered eye sockets like Lauren Bacall used to.

Sometimes I think I'm waiting for him to offer to teach me to whistle and then I'll teach him a thing or two. Sometimes he just makes me feel old and stupid. Sometimes I look over at his slim hips in his tight Guess jeans and feel like the Pillsbury Dough Boy. And sometimes, when I move his hardened hair out of his eye for him he looks up at me from lowered sockets, and I think that he thinks of me as a father figure.

And then I want to die.

All of this has led to a crisis with Dina. The fact that Thor was kissing some other man in that car. The fact that Heloise quit and ran off to an island, because I'd lost my god-given ability to decorate because Thor was kissing that man in that car. The fact that Benny stopped speaking to me after I refused to give him the job that Heloise vacated after I lost my god-given talent after I saw Thor two-timing me with that other guy in that car. The fact that I get a little cutie in the job that I didn't give to Benny for which he is not speaking to me, which Heloise ran away from screaming because I dared do back-to-school because my brain had been addled by seeing my Thor in that BMW with the geek. And the fact that I've kept my hands off the cutie and every other cutie, because my heart's been mashed by the facts that: I am old and FAT; Heloise, who I had trusted and trained in the ways of suggestive sales has left me; Benny cared more for the job than he did for me; and Thor cared more for the other guy than for me, who had been following him faithfully for weeks, just like a little puppy, who followed ten paces back and ducked into dress shops at the mere suggestion of an over-the-shoulder glance.

All of this lead to a crisis with Dina. Because she could do NOTHING to help me.

I walked into her office on a Tuesday afternoon. She was wearing black and watering a new fern that hung from one of her exposed beams. "I feel I should warn you," she said, "that I feel I'm coming out of my earth tones and am moving closer to black." She knows the importance of fashion in my life and gives me ample warnings.

I poured my heart out to her as she brewed rose hip tea. I told her about Thor and the car. Told her of his betrayal. And used the word: betrayal.

"Wyatt," she said, and I knew from the softness of her voice that she was going to say something that she considered to be profound. She always speaks very very softly when she is being profound. So that I'll have to stop tapping or rapping and pay close attention to her to hear the words.

"Wyatt," she said softly, "Have you asked this man,

this . . . Thor . . . just what his feelings are for you? Can he betray you without first making some sort of emotional vow?"

That was all I needed to hear. Dina gets more like my mother every day. She's even starting to purse her lips.

So I haven't seen her in weeks. And haven't spoken to Benny for what seems like months. Until today. When he came into my office, which is why I'm writing again, why I can live with hope.

With the summer heat behind us, I was teaching Byron to do dried-flower and wicker-figure displays in celebration of the Druid ritual of harvest. I am training him as self-lessly as I did Heloise, and am beginning to feel a bit reborn in my work, as I received many kind words over my back-to-school display.

And Benny comes running into my office. He glared at Byron, who fixed one of his smiles right back at Benny. When the smile didn't work, Byron, not knowing the circumstances as to why this older man was immune to his charms, asked to go to lunch. He left and Benny paced the room a bit, fidgeting with some dried blossoms.

"I've missed you," I said finally.

And Benny started in. On how he hadn't missed me because he'd been at work this whole time for my benefit, and so felt that I was nearby every moment. On how he'd followed this other man from the car, having seen him and his BMW again in the mall parking lot. How he knew that there was hope for me with Thor because the man lived in a condo and had one of those wouldn't-you-just-know-it names, Randy, and worked in a boring office.

This information in and of itself might have been enough to send me back to the third floor of the mall once again to wait for Thor at David's Cookies, but Benny had more to say.

"I've found out a way to uncover this Randy's every

deep dark secret,'' Benny said to me, his eyes bulging with pleasure. ''I've found out where he takes his exercise class and I have seen him naked.''

Just imagine my joy, dear diary.

10

November 17

Dear Diary,

I guess that I should have seen it coming, but I didn't. Byron's defection. I should have guessed it from the first moment in which he began spending his spare time over in men's wear. And when he became so chummy with Ron Pratt. Lunches together. Lunches that always went fifteen minutes over the allotted hour. But I said nothing.

But I didn't fail to notice that Byron began to dress like Ron — those overly loose clothes that come with two or three layers of shoulder pad built right in. Ron's the sort that spends a good fifty percent of his income right here at the store. One of the ones that I suspect only works in retail in order to get a twenty percent discount.

So I should have noticed right away that Byron's attentions were turning away from suggestive sales. But I was taken totally by surprise when he told me that he wanted to transfer to men's furnishings for the Christmas rush. I pointed out that I, too, needed extra help at Christmas and that it was truly the best time of the year for retail display, what with all the trees to trim and all. I even promised him his own tree, but he just smiled his blond little smile and said, "You wouldn't want to hold me back, would you?"

And I'll be damned if it didn't work in the end, which left me running around with the measuring tape around MY neck and no help in sight.

Which is when I went down to gift wrap just in time to see Benny getting lessons in seasonal bows. And just in time to see the pitiful look on his face as he wove the red ribbon and the green ribbon. Which is when I decided that I really did need the help and that Benny really was much too creative for gift wrap, which really consists of gold paper with the store name on it and clear tape and red and green bows, when I could open him up to a world of colored lights and spectacular suggestive sales formats. Give him his own tree, even.

Which is why I broke down and hired him in the end. Or transferred him, really, which is always a hell of a lot easier than bringing in someone from the outside. Which is frowned upon in that everyone who is from "outside" is considered to be a wetback or worse.

So they let me hire — transfer — Benny into display and hired some wetback for gift wrap.

And I do have to say that he is working out just fine. Really. He comes to work these days wearing a black turtleneck and a beret, in that I've given him his own display area. Back in the rear of furniture. He's transformed the area into "A Christmas in Paris." All blue lights and twisted wire and foil ornaments and colored cellophane over all. I've never seen him work so hard. Our only angry words were over my refusal to let him smoke those little thin cigars while at work. He wants "to smoke like Alexis." That's what he says. And he insists that Alexis is not passé.

But what is best is that he keeps me up to date on Randy and the exercise class. He says that the class is very good and that other than himself and Randy there is only one man in the group. And that the other man is prematurely balding, but still very cute, and who he thinks is interested in him in that the balding man stands behind him during the toe touching.

He also says that Randy is the only man he's ever known who has cellulite and that he can't believe that Thor would be truly involved with him. Because Benny's seen him naked and says that no man would curl up with Randy, who Benny describes as being shaped "like a placenta."

All of which does my heart good and would probably earn Benny his job even if he weren't doing "Christmas in Paris."

I have not attended the class as yet, in that it is Christmas rush and I work from dawn to dusk flocking things in artificial snow and tying velvet ribbons around plaster busts. Christmas is the one time of year in which I tend to be more traditional in my work, although I do tend to blend shades of the colors red and green that no man has blended before.

In two weeks' time, my major work will be done. All that will remain will be the replacing of ornaments as they are purchased. And then my life can return to normal, and I will get to enjoy the sight of Byron and Ron Pratt standing trapped behind a sales counter while dozens of umbrella-armed women try to buy underwear for all the men on their lists. Then I'll have my revenge.

Then I'll go back to Dina's office — she still calls me every Wednesday just to see how I am and to find out why I missed my session on Tuesday.

I say that the pain of her betrayal — taking Thor's side in his parking-lot betrayal — still stings too much for me to see her, most especially if she is still wearing black and has not returned to earth tones. But I know that I will see her soon. And that we will drink hot tea against the snow/rainy afternoon. And that we will talk and again we shall understand everything there is to understand.

And I know that then, after having again returned to Dina, as well as after having dropped the necessary twelve pounds, I will go to Fitness World with Benny and join him and Randy and the balding man and Arlene the instructor and all the girls for a foray into fitness that Arlene calls "Sweat It Out." '

11

I have to get all stream of consciousness here. It is the Christmas season and, in retail, panic is everywhere. What if they don't buy anything? What if they buy everything too soon and there is nothing left to sell?

The mall is crowded with more and more people every day. If they'd all just lie down at once, it would look like the fall of Atlanta. I pick through the crowds on my break, on my lunch hour. Thor is nowhere to be found. Not in the coffee shop, not in the newsstand. Not in any of the other places in which I've seen him before.

On one bleak afternoon, I thought for a moment that I saw him looking at a Christie Brinkley swimsuit calendar in Waldenbooks, but it turned out to be just another slightly balding man with a paunch, and not MY slightly balding man with a paunch.

At the store, Benny is very much caught up with not just the holiday season and spirit, but also with the idea of display in general and changing all the displays I've done for the last two months.

He runs through the store with that damned tape

measure around his neck, never looking to the left, never looking to the right, his knees kicking out slightly in opposite directions. He has taken to wearing fisherman sweaters, and, I am quite sure, although I cannot prove it, a vague trace of eyeshadow.

He insists that he has never been in such good shape as he is now that he is involved in Sweating It Out. I have promised to join in in the first week of January, if I should happen to lose the necessary weight. Benny says that this is like cleaning before the maid comes. I do not argue the point with him, but I have been doing sit-ups in quiet moments. But I don't tell Benny about this.

Because I hate Benny Roshomon.

But this is not the reason that I haven't told him about the sit-ups. It is because Dina always told me that I was a little anal, a bit compulsive. Just because, when I saw the movie *Ordinary People,* I had an argument with her — a violent argument, mind you — because I saw nothing wrong with Mary Tyler Moore being upset with Donald Sutherland's not being concerned about what socks he wore to their son's funeral. I thought then — and still do, to be honest — that it is perfectly rational to be interested in accessorizing properly to show respect for the dead.

Dina took it to mean that, if I had a cleaning woman, I would dust the day before she came, so as not to have her think me sloppy. This may well be true, but I would rather die than admit it to Dina.

As you can see, they think alike, Benny and Dina.

And I hate her, too. I hate Dina Dutchman. In her earth-toned room with her aromatic tea.

To tell the truth, I suspect that Benny is now seeing Dina. He's beginning to talk just like her. The other day, he told me that my behavior was "not appropriate." He could only be getting that sort of stuff from Dina. And I think that's where the fisherman sweaters are coming from, too. She would suggest something like a fisherman sweater — all tan and lumpy.

It is all too perfect — Benny sitting across that polished oak table from Dina, the fern of Damocles hanging over his head for a change. And he's pouring out his heart to her and paying his bill with the money he's earning from the job that I gave him. Sometimes I feel like following him to her office and bursting in shouting, "My god! My wife! My best friend!" But I wouldn't know who was which, so I don't do it. Besides, Dina would smile slightly and Benny would call my behavior "inappropriate" and Dina would make tea and then I'd be back to Tuesdays at six.

I probably could use the help, too, but the temptation to put my head down on the polished oak table and weep weep weep would be just too great.

And it's Christmas time. Just when I thought things couldn't get worse — what with Benny and Dina cheating on me behind my back and Thor kissing Randy in the parking garage and my traveling pain honing in on the stomach/sinus meridian, Christmas has to happen to me. And then I picture Dina and Benny roasting a turkey and Thor and Randy toasting champagne and me at home watching the Alistair Sim version of *A Christmas Carol* for the tenth time or the colorized *It's a Wonderful Life* for the first . . . and then the traveling pain travels to the vicinity of my heart.

Not that I feel sorry for myself. Oh, no. Yesterday, although bogged down by my hours of holiday retail work and my traveling pain and my deceitful friends, I made my way to the home of a psychic that Pixie told me about.

Pixie told me about this psychic just before she told me that she intends to go off on a Christmas ski vacation with a married man, who she insists is going to be divorced right after the holidays. This not only worries me as to the sanity of my friend Pixie for believing such things, but gives me a feeling of desertion and separation anxiety on top of everything else.

Anyway, so I call and make an appointment and then actually keep this appointment with this psychic, this woman named Fauna, right? I go to an apartment building that looks like the Volvos that they used to make in the early sixties, and come face to face, at the apartment door, with a big brass door knocker. It was shaped like a lion's head. Anyway, I knocked with the knocker.

"I have that on my door because I'm a Leo," she said as she opened the door — quite sure that I'd been staring at the thing, which I was, as there was nothing else on the door to look at to be very Holden Caulfield about the whole thing.

To be even more stream of consciousness for a moment, I must emphasize that I, for a very long time, empathized with Holden Caulfield and felt that he and he alone might have understood me, although I never, for the life of me, understood why he fled from the tender arms of his former English teacher. But other than that, Holden was pretty much put together as I felt I was put together. Dina sighs when I quote him.

Anyway, after the lion's head has been removed from my view by the swinging of the door, I am face to face with a thin thin woman with the reddest hair I have ever seen. And a purple jumpsuit and one of those apple-seed necklaces that were popular back when those Volvos were being made. The kind of necklaces that everyone was always warned not to chew on because they were supposed to be poison. But no one ever knew whether or not they were really poison, because no one ever chewed on them to find out.

Anyway, this redhead has a jaw on her like you've never seen before. And she gives me orange juice and sits me down on this living-room couch — a nice brown leather couch covered with a sheet — and starts in on me. My lover is untrue. There will be a change in my job in the coming year. I will see new horizons. My Mars is square Scorpio in my second house. She tells me things like that.

For a long while, I am not having a good time. Or believing a word she says. For instance, my lover is not just untrue, he is nonexistent. But then I tell her of my out-of-body experiences. She takes my hand for a long moment and then gets me more juice. When she returns, she is beaming. She says that my gift is true. That I have this great gift of freeing my spirit from my body and that I must use this gift to increase my wisdom and my understanding of the Nature of the Universe. I don't, by this time, know if it's the juice or the sitar music or that woman's jaw, but I'm beginning to believe her. Then she tells me that I must take care not to tear the silver cord — that which connects my soul to my body — when I travel. And she asks me if I have read any of Shirley MacLaine's books.

I tell her that I haven't, but that I have visited Moscow recently. At least I thought it was Moscow, because all the words were made up of little squiggles instead of letters. She said that it might have been somewhere in Arabia because all their letters looked more like little squiggles than the Russian letters do. But I told her that I saw snow there, so we both agreed that I was probably in Moscow and she was very impressed.

Then she blessed me by rubbing sunflower oil on my forehead. I told her about the traveling pain, and she said that she could help me with that if I'd burn sacred sage for incense and would hold a crystal to the pained part of my body when it was in pain. I told her I would try it and then she said she thought that she could see me Tuesdays at six.

As I walked to my car, I passed a Christmas tree on someone's lawn. It was lit with outdoor lights. All blue. And I remembered that my Aunt Della, my one and only rich relative, had lit her tree with blue lights and that the tree had filled me with a terrible melancholy and a feeling that I would never understand the ways of the sophisticated rich, both at once. And I stood there on the sidewalk looking at this awful terrible depressing little tree, beset as it was with blue lights, and I, the display expert, just crumpled. It all came rushing back, all the things I had to fear and hate: Dina and Benny and the job and the mall and the season and the memory that filled me from earmuffs to snowboots with heat. Heat and rage. The image of those two men locked in a happy embrace during the heat of summer.

And then it came back. The pain, the terrible pain. And it traveled through every avenue of my body, through veins, through arteries, to every inch of my being. And the sorrow that went through me, as I walked to my car clutching against the pain that grew and traveled in me anyway, the sorrow that went through me, you don't know. You don't even know.

12

You need to know about Benny Roshomon. Because, like the African drumbeats in a Tarzan movie, his presence is felt even if you can't quite see where it is coming from. In fact, like African drumbeats, Benny Roshomon often seems to be all around you.

And I know what you're thinking. I get this a lot, in fact Dina asked me the first time I mentioned Benny. Why am I friends with him? And that's easy to answer. When I first met him about four or five years ago, I couldn't help but think that he was interesting. He was, at that time, trying to make a go of it as a professional apache dancer with a particularly homely but very very thin woman called Franseen. No last name.

They were at that time pulling down some money for their act at the gay bars in the area, performing an act called "Passionne au Deux," which involved a good bit of Benny flinging Franseen to the ground and then slapping her face when he helped her back to her feet. But you know the bars — after two weeks they were considered to be passé and trios of singing black girls became the next "thing."

Benny suggested that they become more tribal, which meant that he intended to be more brutal to Franseen. He wanted to refer to the act as "snuff dancing," but here Franseen drew the line and went off to become a word processor.

And it was about this time that Benny first got wind of Phillip Glass and Laurie Anderson and decided to become a performance artist. For this enterprise, his partner was a bald German woman called Gudrun. In front of a set that consisted of blow-up drawings taken from *Grey's Anatomy.* Benny read from John Updike's novel *Rabbit, Run* while Gudrun played the saw. They called this work, "Hare Apparent," and it brought Benny his greatest success, when he was invited to perform this act as part of a PBS special on performance art. Gudrun later told me that Laurie Anderson herself came up to the two of them at the taping and told them that they may as well give up in that they lacked the substance that their act needed in order to be seriously considered "performance."

Benny was undaunted by this and insisted that Laurie Anderson had become "Middle America," a slur if there ever was one. Gudrun, however, was exceedingly daunted by Anderson's curt dismissal of their work, and allowed her hair to grow back in, changed her name to its native Susan and became a word processor.

It was at this point that Benny discovered Dada, an art process through which he could conclude that nothing meant anything and that he could prove this through everything he did.

Benny continued with Dada until the day he became a gift wrapper. He performed a series of innovations that he entitled "Final Affects." These involved a number of defunct car parts — flat tires and broken radios chief among them — and spray paint and a sledge hammer.

He performed the numbers solo, hammering the car parts while chanting the poetic words of black feminists. "Ego Tripping" was his big number.

And going solo proved Benny's greatest fear. For he hit the skids on the arts circuit. Where he and Franseen were considered to be "cute," "a divertisement," and Gudrun and he were, for a brief moment until Laurie Anderson spoke her opinion in front of the director and crew of the PBS special, to say nothing of the other performance artists present, all of whom gossiped like mad, well, they were considered kind of "cutting edge," and certainly serious about their work. Who else could even read *Rabbit, Run,* much less chant portions of it out loud over and over again?

But Benny alone was considered obtuse. Jejune. Grants were withdrawn. And the leftist press turned its back upon his Dadaist meanderings. Worst of all, those who still wrote about him at all or mentioned him referred to him as being very "seventies." Even his taking to wearing nothing but the color black didn't help after someone mentioned that it was "just like Johnny Cash."

And so Benny turned his attention to gift wrap, first as a Dada experiment and then as a career move. And then he became my assistant — and I use the term in a very Eve Harrington way — and began to try to steal my analyst.

So, why is he my friend?

Well, as I've already said, when I first met him, I found

him fascinating. Remember, at the time, his face or quoted words were on the cover of every periodical with a circulation under 2,500. And then, upon realizing that I was on his good side and hearing what he had to say about those who were not on that good side, I decided that it was wise to become his friend.

I think that there was a mutual attraction also. A sexual attraction. Within a week or two of our first meeting, he invited me over to his loft for dinner. I arrived at the scheduled hour to find that he wasn't even home yet. I sat down on the top step of the four flights that I'd climbed to reach his apartment and ran my fingers over the black ribbed vinyl runner that covered the steps.

He came home an hour later and let me in. NO apologies. He gave me a can of clamato juice and showed me around. It was a large, almost totally vacant room with bits of neon all over the walls. This was the only real lighting. In the center of the room was a teeter-totter, upon which he insisted we sit. "It makes power plays much more direct," he said.

And so I sat down and I spent the next twenty minutes begging him to let me down. Suddenly I was eight years old and on the playground again. By the time he did let my feet touch the ground, there was no doubt in my mind that we would sleep together.

But we did manage to stay friends of a sort. Mostly because every time I reached my limit with him, he'd lower his jaw and look up at me through intense eyes — I realize now that he was imitating Lauren Bacall, but I was younger then — and say, "Cleave Unto Me. . . ."

For some reason, this always worked. I did cleave. But I never slept with him. Which had the final result of keeping me from having a satisfying sexual relationship, while giving me the ongoing ordeal of a tormented intense relationship in its place. It wasn't until I began seeing Dina regularly that I began not minding that Benny sleeps around like a mad dog in heat. And that I began to think that I myself deserved a little fun of my own. It was at this moment that I first laid eyes upon the man that I've now been hunting for the last six months. And it was the fact that this man looked to be Benny's opposite number, right down to the thinning blond hair and the clean clean skin, that I became interested.

And that's the truth of the situation.

But you must understand that for some reason — one that neither of us really understand — there is a bond between Benny and me. Along the way, I have always encouraged his works — in fact, I was the one who suggested that he get involved with jewelry design. And he did, at that time, turn out a rather profitable number of rings and bracelets featuring marbles — cats-eyes chief among them — as their centerpieces. And I was the one who involved him in his interior designs. For this reason: that there are a number of homes and offices in our area that could be bettered by having jungle gym equipment in them.

And for his part, Benny has always given my life the excitement that it sorely lacked before he came along. But, more important than this, Benny was the one who made me realize that a man who wanted to sleep with other men was simply a man who wanted to sleep with other men and not a demon or a sick son of a bitch. Until I met Benny, I realize now that I went about with an imaginary black rectangle across my eyes and lower forehead. Like a person photographed in scandal sheets. But Benny ripped off that rectangle and that's the sort of action that makes someone your friend for life, no matter what else they do along the way.

So, all of this makes me look at Benny through a camera lens covered with gauze. When he tries to usurp my job or win Dina over to his side, I chant to myself, "He must have

a reason. He surely has a good reason." And then I picture
him in my office, wooing back Byron to be his assistant in
more ways than one. And I imagine him sitting across from
Dina, sipping herbal tea and hearing her say, "Wildroot was
certainly lucky to have a friend like you," and slowly lick-
ing her lips after saying this. And I then find myself in my
imagination again of a hot summer night and I am again
standing behind the car watching Thor kiss — passionately
kiss — another man. And then the two heads part, and I
see that the man is Benny Roshomon.

And I know then that Benny Roshomon is a demon and
a sick son of a bitch.

13

About five years ago, I was driving down a road. It was
one of those long low roads in Florida. The kind that have
dirt shoulders that are wider than the actual lanes. The road
was two lanes wide in each direction, with a concrete
divider in the middle. Behind me were about ten miles of
straight line. Ahead was about five more miles and then a
causeway that would take me in a straight line across the
shallow waters of the Gulf of Mexico.

The road was called Wildcat Drive.

I want to be able to say that I was driving a '59 Thunder-
bird with fins and big foam dice. But what I was driving
was a Pinto station wagon, the kind that had fake wood
panels on each door.

I was driving to meet a friend for lunch. I was on vacation and in that friend's car.

I had a cassette player on the seat next to me, playing loud. This was because I had the windows down and the car's radio was broken. I was listening to Patsy Cline on the cassette deck.

And I had just driven past one of those shabby motels that spring up near large bodies of water, when I heard what sounded like an explosion. And everything happened fast — the car swung of its own volition first toward the concrete divider and then, after I swung my weight on the steering wheel away from the wall, across two lanes of traffic and onto the dirt shoulder. All the while I was braking gently, trying to get the car under some sort of control.

Finally, I jammed my foot onto the brake and the car lurched to a halt, the front end pushed into a ditch, the car sideways to the road.

I was fine, but my forehead rested against the steering wheel. And it rested there a long time before I could convince it to rise. And I slowly looked around the inside of the car at all the objects. The tape, the books, sunglasses, and other stupid vacation toys.

In a minute more, I would be out of the car and be looking at the tire that burst, just burst in the heat. And a few minutes after that, I would have walked back to that motel and would be calling AAA to pull the car out and change the tire. And about an hour later, I would arrive only about twenty minutes late for my lunch and would excuse myself by saying that the car had had a flat tire.

But in the moment that I raised my forehead, I heard music. I heard Patsy Cline still singing "Walking after Midnight," although the cassette was on the floor of the passenger's side of the car. The music continued as if nothing were wrong, although its source, like everything else in my life, lay scattered.

Now, most people would say that I was, in that one moment, discovering my own mortality. But what I was finding was something stranger. I was finding that it would be possible for me to slip out of this life and have the music just keep right on playing. That no one might notice that I was gone. That someone, some paramedic, would come and have to press the button of the cassette player and turn off the music that my hand had started by punching the same button.

Why I am telling this, I'm not sure. But I attest to the fact that, in the last five years, I have not managed to push myself past the moment that I first noticed that music — not as I walked up that road to the motel, or as I discussed the memory with Dina. And not, four Christmases later, as I prepared to celebrate the fifth.

14

I have feelings. Oh, a whole brass band of feelings. One more set of memories before we hurry ahead.

Because there's something I haven't mentioned yet. Someone who puts everything into perspective.

I have to think back to my early twenties, which is, I realize, an oblique admission that I am indeed Over Thirty. It's true. But it is also true that most people think that I am about twenty-seven. Some even guess as low as twenty-five. But only on foggy nights or by candlelight.

But there was a time — oh, God, it was now a decade ago — when I was finishing off my college years, quietly majoring in art history with a group of girls in granny dresses and smocks. This was healing for me, smarting as I still was about Rollo. Pixie was with me still, and wearing a smock.

But I was something of a Friar in college and tended to lean against trees for comfort and support. I did, however, manage one night to go to a theater-in-the-round production of the outstanding works of Kaufman and Hart, as performed by the drama department, and happened to sit next to a rather odd-looking tall student with next to no eyes and an unusually large nose.

I would be sitting next to him for the better part of the next seven years.

Of course, for much of that time, I would blame him for most of the world's ills, like others do Hitler and LBJ. But the years have tempered my feelings on the subject, and now, philosophically, I remind myself that first love, like the first version of anything else, shows all the seams and rough edges that later practice will learn to hide.

I do, however, still hold with the fact that names give away more than we think they do, and that the nasty nasal whine of his name should have warned me from the first moment of just what I was getting into.

Sean — is there a whinier syllable anywhere? I don't think so. Is there an odder name than this trompe-l'oeil number that you can't even pronounce the way it looks?

But, what are you going to do? I looked him square in the face and that was that.

In those early years, he always dressed like a huge seven-year-old. With sneakers and jeans and sweaters and nylon zip-up jackets and a book bag over the left shoulder.

From the first, I guess that, because of our mutual interest in theater — his for acting, mine for design — I saw us working together always. I would create some surroundings, a great palette for him to color. His Hamlet in my Denmark.

But it didn't work out that way. What does? Still, on the nights when we weren't fighting, I would sometimes fit my head in between his chin and shoulder and allow myself to dream.

See, why this is important for you to know is not for the specifics of the relationship — just know that it was of the sort that the bleach-blond boys in tight pants shriek about and wave their arms in the air over, with all the arguments in restaurants and trying to run each other down with cars, etc. — but for you to be aware that there WAS this relationship and that I haven't spent my whole life moving these big dolls around and dressing and undressing them. Although Sean, even after all these years, would raise one eyebrow and strongly question my last sentence.

Now, this relationship did many things to and for me. But among them was letting loose the dogs of war. In other words, some door opened in my brain that made me see out-of-work-actors more clearly than I do any other people. And they see me pretty damned clearly, too — I think in the image of their mother, dressed just as their mother dressed, holding a steaming platter of their favorite food. In fact, I think I must be listed in some actor's guidebook somewhere, as an easy touch.

But, in terms of love, Sean was the first. Even though he never shaved — I gave up shaving just to fit in with him. Even though he was a slob — I stopped picking up his clothes and threw mine on the floor next to his. Even though he was a moody son of a bitch — I learned to stop staring at people like a frightened marsupial and to plant myself and scream at the top of my lungs.

This is why I tell you this: this experience was the one in which I realized how well two people can come to know each other — that you can pick out the sound of their sleep-breathing from that of anyone else. That you can know the back of their neck so well, and feel like crying every time you see it, because it looks so vulnerable. That you can worry about someone more than you do about yourself, and sit up waiting if they're late, just like your parents used to do for you. That there can be another person who shares your whole life, that when you can't pay the rent, they say well, now, just don't worry and then put money on the spot on the bed between where you're both sitting.

Because that's what this is about. It's about the moment when someone looks me in the face and says, "Wyatt," and knows what they're talking about. . . .

Which is not to say that my relationship with Sean ended easily or well. We clomped along for years. We would argue and I would run home to Pixie. Or he would go stay with his best friend, Brian, a music major with little round glasses. And then we would make up and it would all be easy again, and I'd wonder why we ever fought until the next time we fought.

And, oh, I graduated and he quit school and went on to be an out-of-work actor professionally. And I ran a bookstore and he went on auditions and didn't get cast. And somehow I came up with the rent and, now that I look back on them, these were incredibly sweet days and weeks and years.

But, at the time, they seemed endless. The ongoing "almost" of Sean's acting career. The rare times in which he got a part and we could celebrate an opening night — always with some other designer's set, as I was too busy working to even think of design. The times that Pixie would come for dinner and we would all settle in with cheap wine and my bad cooking and she wouldn't once seem upset or surprised at two men who treated each other as if they were married.

And then Pixie one day let me know as softly as she

could, for I had had another fight with Sean and was sleeping on the floor of her living room, that she had a new job and was moving back East to take it.

And then Sean one day let me know loudly that he had had it with me and my lousy cooking and his lack of work and that he, too, was moving back East to become famous.

And so, for a few weeks, I moved books around the shelves of the bookshop. And then I called Pixie and asked her if I could stay on her East Coast living room floor until I could get myself settled. And she said yes.

I don't really know just what I had in mind— but like Little Eva on the ice floes, I fled the Midwest forever. I think on some subconscious level, I felt that Sean and I would pick up where we left off. After all, with all the time we'd been together, I felt, when he left, as if someone had hacked off my left leg and mailed it to Alaska. In my mind, I was just going off to reclaim my leg.

And he didn't seem surprised when I called to say, guess what?, I was coming East. Although he might have been less pleased to learn that I was to be living in a different city. But we, I guess you could say we dated. One would travel to see the other and we'd have overly polite meals in restaurants.

After a few months of this, I finally got around to asking Sean the thing that I'd never wanted to know — whether or not he'd ever slept with Brian, the music major. I asked him one day during one of those phone conversations that you can only have with someone with whom you've lived, but with whom you live no longer. The way that I guess people talk after they've been through a "good divorce." We were just chatting away about how our days were filling themselves and how we had made the best decision all the way around, what with these brand new lives of ours and our new relationship as true and understanding friends, and I said, "Sean, there's something that I always wondered about, and I hope that you'll tell me truthfully now that we're such true and understanding friends but did you ever sleep with Brian, the music major?''

And the bastard admitted that he had. Over and over again.

Well, they say that fatal illness has five stages to it and I say so does divorce. And the longest and best is the stage in which you hate their fucking guts and you wish you had used the bread knife when you had the chance. When you think of all the times that they were sleeping next to you, trusting and helpless. And you did nothing!

After the conversation, I realized that, by the time Sean and Wyatt became a thing of the past, dear old Wyatt was crowding thirty, while that son of a bitch cocksucking lowlife scum of the earth no-talent Sean was just twenty-five. Twenty-five and loosed upon the casting couches of the Mid-Atlantic states.

Well, I tried bars. But they don't work for me. I mean, I haven't, I guess, described myself fully to you, but let's just say that I'm someone that you have to get to know in order to love. It's my warmth, my unique view of the world, my standing with my arms akimbo that will win you over, not my body — never my body. So the bars, what with all the muscle shirts and beer, never were my venue.

So I tried therapy for the first time. Group therapy for gay men. The group was run by a gay man. We all gave false names, I'm sure. I said my name was Bill. And that helped for a little while, until one of the other members of the group was won over by my warmth and my akimboed arms and started inviting me to go dancing after group therapy. And, like a fool, I went, because, let's face it, I only went to group in the first place to learn why I couldn't meet men, so if I met one in the group I'd be crazy to turn him down, right? So I didn't, and, when the group leader found out, we both got kicked out of group for dating within the group, which we had been forbidden to do.

It was at this low ebb about two years ago that I solved two issues. First, I got this job doing floor displays for a major department store — and I was thrilled at the prospect of using my design talents, but more, I was thrilled at the prospect of having a design assistant. Instant boy, I figured — who ever heard of a design assistant who wouldn't sleep with his master? But as you know, it doesn't work that way. You run through them like you do socks. They come, they go. But they never seem to come with me. Except one named the archetypal gay name — Bruce. Bruce had eyes that looked in opposite directions, but he had an air of youth about him. I used to lay him across the table in the design office, among the dried flowers and mannequin parts. But the police picked him up one day for grand theft auto and I got a new assistant. And then another and another. . .until now there's Benny, who told me this morning that he was working on the concept of a new one-man show called *The Seven Ages of Elvis,* which blends Shakespeare and Elvis, the Bard and the King. Benny says that he's going to play all the parts, from the skinny young Elvis the Pelvis through the final fat white jump-suited Las Vegas Elvis. Maybe the act will catch on and he'll have a big success. And then I can get myself another Bruce and start throwing him across the design table.

Maybe Benny will end up on TV like Sean, who I see all the time now on *The Guiding Light,* and whose face I saw looking out at me while I was on line at the supermarket from the cover of one of those soap magazines. I didn't buy it. I didn't want to know.

The other big decision I made two years ago? Dina, of course. The bitch, the cocksucking scum-of-the-earth tramp, tart, no talent.

And I really kind of miss her.

15

Tomorrow is Christmas Eve. And I begin to reflect on life.

As I reflect on life, more and more I liken it to skipping stones across the surface of a lake.

Picture it: it is sunny. A hot and sunny day. The lake's surface seems almost rigid; pulled taut. It is calm and reflective and shows the sunlight above, but also the cooler shadows of the willows that overhang the water's surface.

This is life, this is our texture, the surface upon which we play.

We are the stones that spin out on the water. Bouncing and dipping, hoping that our momentum will pitch us far before we fall. The whole point seems to be twofold: to get as far out onto the lake as possible before sinking (for the area below the water's surface is death, the unknown, from which no skipping stone has ever returned), and to make as many ripples on the water's surface as possible and have them last as long as possible. By the ripples, by the disruptions of the water's flat face, we are remembered and someone always says, "Look at the beautiful ripples." Or, "the wonderful swirls."

Unless, of course, there is reincarnation, and then the stones, over the course of years and years, find their way back to the water's edge and then back out onto dry land, through whatever mysterious process Nature uses to perform such tasks, and then other hands will pick up the stones and toss them across the water, and other voices will echo, "Such a beautiful ripple."

These are the things about which I think, after these weeks with Fauna. And while waiting for my Christmas miracle.

16

It's time for the Christmas part of my story. The part that makes the movie musical adaptation of my story possible. Only they'll change things a bit — add a happy middle-class family somehow. I'll end up the father of twelve and a widower who sees a mystery woman on Christmas Eve, only to fall in love with her, but to lose her when he must leave his twelve children and go off to war, in which he's crippled but only temporarily — blinded, maybe — but he regains his sight on the next Christmas Eve when he and his children attend services at midnight at the Cathedral; and the very first sight he sees as his vision begins to return, blurry at first, and then sharper and sharper until he sees the first image — is the mystery woman standing in front of him, her scarf still dampened by the snow, and then she tells him that she loves him and has loved him for this long and lonely year but knows that they'll be together — all fourteen of them — for the rest of their long and happy lives. Fade out.

However, on this Christmas Eve, I managed to leave the store early, after having moved the few decorations left to the front of the once-tastefully decorated artificial trees, so that the scavengers and losers could buy what was left at thirty percent off.

I went to keep my appointment with Fauna. And it was on this day that we talked about two things that Dina had pretty much made me feel were behind me for good. First there was the Traveling Pain. Dina said that this was Guilt, Guilt and more Guilt. Fauna said it was Karma, which was not to be talked out, but was, rather, to be worked out by paying back in this lifetime the people I'd harmed in past lifetimes. When I asked for more details, Fauna smiled at me with the quizzical half-smile that she'd taken to smiling since the third or fourth time I'd come to see her, and said that the answers weren't within her, but were within me.

Then she said that while she was at it, she wanted me to know that Dina was all wrong about my out-of-body experiences, too. That they were not the product of Rejection, Rejection and more Rejection, but were, rather, just my spirit's natural playfulness at work. And that I should go and soar and have a good time, but just be careful not to twist or rend in any way my silver cord. I asked her what the silver cord was and she said that it was the umbilical cord that tied my spirit to my body and didn't I remember seeing it when I floated off in the past? I said, no, that when I floated off in the past, I'd just sort of popped out and gone off to the mountains or somewhere not charted very clearly on the map.

She said I was a natural psychic and just to be careful of my cord.

It was along about this time that I couldn't help but notice that Fauna was getting ready to go somewhere, what with the fact that she'd put on lipstick and earrings while I was talking to her. And then she held out two dresses in front of me, one a blue and green number that should have had the word "Vera" written in one corner, and the other a black one that was slit up to the waistline, and asked me which I liked better.

For her or for me, I asked her, and she pursed her magenta lips at me. Dina never behaved this way. Or had magenta lips.

Then she told me that I could only find happiness that night in my own backyard, just like the old song said. Either that, or I could go to the party with her.

I said no thanks, but asked her a few questions just to keep her psychic waters flowing. She answered me mostly monosyllabically. Then I asked, "Fauna, why is it that I feel so lost, so restless, so brokenhearted?"

I expected a long answer. I expected her to tell me that my Karma was gummed up by the lifetime in which I was a sultan, or something. But she only smiled and said, "Wildroot, honey, everyone gets a little down at Christmas."

And then she gave me some presents: a little black notebook, a little silver pencil, and a rock crystal that came with a sheet of instructions. Then she kissed me good night as we walked out the door and she went off to her party.

Outside, it was snowing. Not too heavily, just enough to be Christmas Eve. There I was walking in front of the Cathedral, and no Van Johnson.

I guess that I got as far as the front door of my apartment house before I turned around and walked back out into the snow. I walked back to the mall, which wasn't far, but wasn't near enough either for any sane man to go walking on Christmas Eve. As I got near the place, I could see the mad flurry around it. It was down to the wire now, boy. The last few moments of this year's shopping season. The old year may have another week left in it, but everything important ends tonight.

I walked in at J. C. Penny's. Past the catalogue sales. Past athletics and the toys, what few were left, and out into the mall. I took the elevator with the glass walls that I usually won't take because of my fear of heights. I went up to the top floor, circled it, walking slowly and went down the steps to the next level.

It was a few minutes before I knew why I was there. That this was my own backyard.

When I say that I walked slowly, I must add that I went with great effort. A salmon upstream. Fighting against a human current that pushed and hurried and bustled and downright ran to get these things home and wrapped for Harry and Mary and Baby. And I just kept on strolling, and being shoved this way and that.

Outside of a card store, the will to move left me and I stood staring into the mob that fought for the last of the tissue paper. I stood and stared until eyes met mine. These eyes, blue-gray and desperately trying to be calm, locked into mine from within stacks and stacks of packages that wiggled to and fro. The eyes worked from a body, however, that had already stepped into my personal space. The collision sent packages flying and, with great apology, I gathered and stacked them to return them to the eyes.

If I have expressed all of this in a most Victorian fashion, it is because I instinctively feel that only the claws of the great Queen herself could get me through this telling.

For, when the packages were stacked and ready to be returned, I looked back at the eyes and saw Thor's eyes, and then Thor's hair and Thor's teeth and his face and neck and chest and body. And he smiled at me with a great hearty smile as I again stacked his arms with his purchases. And when that was done, and when we'd paused as long as we tastefully could, just when I was working over the nerve from my stomach to heart to brain to mouth to suggest that we go and get some coffee, Thor winked once with a gray-blue eye and said in a voice textured with silk and burlap, "Well, Merry Christmas."

How long it took him to walk away from me I could never tell you. Only that he did. He walked away. And I kept myself rigid, planted, weighted down in time and space to keep myself from rushing to him, again scattering his packages and then covering his warm face and body with my most fervent, most heartfelt kisses. And then say, "Merry Christmas, Van Johnson."

Not wanting to go home, I went ahead to Pixie's. Where I knew she'd be and I'd be welcome, since her damned married boyfriend had decided that he belonged with his wife on Christmas.

She opened the door wearing an old pink bathrobe, her hair already in curlers, although it was still very early evening. We sat on the couch, my arm around her shoulder, her arm around my waist, and waited for it all to be over.

17

"*B*wana *Wild! Bwana Wild! You go now. Quick like antelope. Drums beat steady. Say bad men come soon I think. We go now."*

"Yes, Benny, we go. But not quite yet." I gave the hapless little toady a gentle shove. It was outside his understanding to know what I looked for. I saw his stomach, huge with its bloat of malnutrition, wobble as he staggered to regain his balance from my love tap. His dirt-smeared face grinned up at me.

"Bad mens come by night."

"Keep going, Benny." I rejoined him. "For we hunt the Goldenhair."

The little native, alarmed and excited by this news, danced his nervous indecision. One more shove and we were going again through the narrow gorge. As we reached the end of it, without a discernable path to follow, I tore free a stout vine from the side of a tree, held Benny safely tucked beneath my left arm and swung us both to a clearing a quarter of a mile away. As we swung and the air pumped in and out of my lungs, I called out, *"Aaahh EEEE Aaahhhhhhhhhhhhhh."*

The multitude of creatures of the jungle turned to look at us as we seemingly flew through the air. It was as if these native life forms, animals and plants, cleared the area in which we landed.

"Make camp, Benny, we stay here tonight."

"But Bwana, bad men come tonight!" Benny looked up at me. His eyes were glazed with fear. Here was my little native companion, so helpless, so savage, so ignorant. It was my burden to protect him and show him the ways of the modern age.

"Let them come, Benny, I don't fear them. Now go and make camp."

I jabbed him playfully on the back of the head, sending him sprawling into the dirt.

I thought of the legend of Goldenhair. Of the wildman feared even by the most vicious native warriors. Of his mane of golden hair that rippled around his wide shoulders. Of the gleam of his tanned body as he leapt fearlessly from high trees, crouched on stout boulders. Of the unearthly snarl that was said to be his only language.

My belief was that he was the child of some missionary couple, whose hearts were braver than their arms. Who, in bringing the modern man's religion to this dark place, *had fallen prey to its inhabitants, leaving a golden youth to grow up alone, and grow up wild.*

I heard drumbeats, insistent, and knew that they had come slightly closer in the passing moments. Knew the natives' trick, that the sound would soon surround me. Let them come, I'd surprises of my own.

A cry of startled panic roused me to action. Standing again bolt upright, my legs spread wide, my hand to my knife, I saw Benny helpless in the grasp of a boa constrictor. Saw his eyes bulging out from their sockets as the giant snake squeezed the life out of him. In a second, I pictured the poor fool tapping the tent pegs with a little rock, ignoring the slowly moving form above him. Imagined the lowering of the snake's dry body and the snaring of Benny's greasy form.

In another second I was at Benny's side. Allowing the snake to enfold me in order to save my little native guide. I felt the pressure of the snake's fierce body. But it felt the strength of my American arms and the sting of my knife.

I pulled the dying reptile off of me. My clothing was so torn by the battle that I was left nearly naked. And I stood there a moment, uncovered and defenseless, as my blade was still embedded in the snake's skull.

It was then that I heard the snarl. Almost before I could turn, I felt the strong, smooth hands upon me, heard Benny's final call, "Goldenhair!" before he fled forever into the jungle.

I forced myself around in his imprisoning arms and looked directly into blue-gray eyes, calm centers in a fierce face. If I could reach those eyes, I knew, I could restore the lost missionary youth.

He, too, was nearly naked, wearing only a slight apron of leaves that left little of his lithe form unexposed. I saw the pounding thrust of his heartbeat, the flow of air into his lungs, the throbbing veins in his throat. The rising bulge that appeared below that apron. His package swung freely as we struggled. And appeared to be growing in power and stature.

Our struggle was titanic. The natives, having heard his savage snarl, ceased their drumbeats. The birds and monkeys stopped their chatter and the jungle was completely silent.

Held fast, almost helpless in his arms, I noticed how very clean was his skin. Noticed the unearthly Pepsodent scent of his breath. His hand moved over my body. He was clean, so very clean.

His hands then traveled my body, rending what remained of my garments and feeling every crevice of my being. My breathing grew deeper, with my growing appreciation of my hopeless state. This was no snake or lion. This one would be my master.

In that moment, all hope left me. I saw myself a moment later, with my vitals ripped free. I gulped.

As he took the back of my now fragile skull in his hands, a snarl again escaped his lips.

And he skimmed my face down his chest and thrust my head into his leaves.

At once, the natives fell to their knees and worshipped and the jungle called out in joy. I felt his fingers bite into the crown of my head, knit into my chestnut hair, as I found and gave rapture between the muscled legs of this wild jungle master.

And the drumbeats again found their rhythm.

18

What do you want? I thought it was the worst idea since *My Mother the Car.* Next thing you know, I'm sitting ringside on New Year's Eve listening to literally dozens of upper-middle-class people just like myself calling Benny's name and applauding loudly. Just like Jerry Lewis in Paris.

And I'm sitting just inches out of the spotlight, Pixie on my left, in what looks like a pink chiffon prom dress; Thallassa, Benny's suspiciously Nazi-esque new agent, on my right, wearing a simple black leather frock festooned with zippers, and I just feel like dying right here and now with my Happy New Year hat attached to my head at a jaunty angle by the rubber band that runs under my chin.

We're in the third or fourth stage of Elvis, I'm not sure which, and Benny is grinding his pelvis for all he is worth.

But let's catch up.

It was seconds ago that Pixie and I embraced on the couch on Christmas Eve, sure that our lives had ended after that married creep refused to take her skiing, and after I had had my chance encounter with the deep blue wells that are Thor's eyes.

We considered a suicide pact, and it was none too soon that one of us noticed that *Desk Set* was on cable, which Pixie has, although my building has yet to be wired, even after more than two years of waiting.

It wasn't until Spencer Tracy told Katherine Hepburn to "never assume," that Pixie and I began to feel better, but slowly the familiar dialogue of bumpy romance brought us both around again to the hopes of a happy ending.

And after that things got smoother.

After all, that week between Christmas Eve and New Year's Eve is only about fifteen minutes long, what with all the food, and the constant need to keep the holiday displays in order against the tide of bargain hunters the day after Christmas.

But it was the Monday after the blessed event that Benny came up to me with two tickets to his show, thrown together at the last minute with the help of his new agent, Thallassa, at the Club Courier. Here Benny had one of his many defeats as a performance artist and here, even as we speak, he is realizing his artistic triumph as a, as he calls it, "Faux Presley."

But this is an evening of fire and ice. Benny has already informed me that, should *The Seven Ages of Elvis* prove to be as thoroughly entertaining as he is sure it will be, then he will be leaving my employ to continue his performances aboard cruise ships and in hotel lounges all across North America. It seems that the chubby little man who gave my hand a clammy little shake early on in the evening is the booking agent for such enterprises. And given the audience's loud approval of Benny's act and Thallassa's apparent ability to overwhelm all comers, I would call Benny's continuing performance a sure bet.

Which may have at one time angered me or hurt me or confused me at the very least, but I, sitting here at the edge of the spotlight, have gazed into the darkness all around.

And there, all in earth tones, I have seen Dr. Dina Dutchman, escorted by the sort of man who plays squash after a day spent selling investment commodities. I have seen them hold hands above the table and watched her lower her head and wreath of soft soft hair against the crook of his neck. They are drinking champagne.

And Benny has not let it end there. In the deeper shadows, the darker reaches, there is a man with thinning blond hair, who, I can see from here, is wearing a suit without wrinkles. And with him is a person — a man, the sort of man which drains all those around him of talent and wit and range and depth. Who makes of those who love him the sort who know the names of wines and who wear thin gold chains around their ankles.

And so everyone I love is in this room, with the people that they love instead of me. And Benny, most of all, is loved by everyone in this fucking place and Thallassa has her hand on my thigh.

But here is numbness and only numbness. Because this is the darkest night. Walpurgisnacht. This is the moment in which Scarlet O'Hara eats her radish. And vows are about to be taken and everything is about to change.

Here am I, Wildroot. Beset with many sorrows. Sitting in the range of light, looking out to where the eyes glitter like wild animals outside the safe spot of the fire.

You see, it is as if Benny had planned it all to crush me. These faces faces faces. But I, in my moment of despair, in which Wildroot nearly slipped away, looked further into the darkness and found liquid, flowing life.

For behind Dina and off to the right of Thor and his pet pig, there in further darkness, in the brilliant instant of lighting a Gitane, I saw the face of Orly Kasaba.

PART TWO

"Always go forward and never turn back."
— Father Junipero Serra

19

When I pointed Orly Kasaba out to Pixie, her reaction was non-verbal, but the fingernail jabs in my left arm led me to believe that she, too, remembered Orly from college and that she was also glad to see him.

"Why don't you go over and ask him to join us?" I suggested to her oh-so-sweetly.

"Why don't you?" she countered, still having not let go of my arm.

"You."

"You."

"You."

It was at this point that Thallassa interrupted us with a look — a look that made us both turn our attention back to the stage on which Benny was singing "In the Ghetto."

We sat in silence for a moment, watching Benny. I was thinking that it was not just that I did not want to have to pass in front of Dina and Thor's tables to get to Orly that held me back, it was also that I was unsure of Orly's taste in men versus women and I wanted to use Pixie as bait. Sort of a *Suddenly Last Summer* motif.

I put my head in her lap and began to moan. "All right," she hissed and slowly rose from the table and began walking over toward Orly, who sat alone, with his black, thick hair pulled back and rippling over the back of his neck. Who smoked his cigarette with a sensuality that nearly embarrased me, most particularly when I considered what I would give him to smoke in the place of his tobacco.

But the moment that Pixie left the table, I knew that I had made a mistake in sending her over to fetch Orly for me. For several reasons. For one, I saw the look on Orly's face when she arrived at his table, a look that did not recognize an old friend, but one that looked at her as if she were a parfait. For another, there was the fact that the two were not hurrying right back to pay attention to me, but she was sitting down at his table and they appeared to be trying to order drinks. And, finally, there was the fact that, with Pixie out of the way, Thallassa was sidling ever closer to me.

I cannot tell you the hatred I felt toward Pixie at that moment. There she was, my oldest friend, joining the cult of duplicity that seemed to have sprung up around my name and image. In the one room, we had a renegade design assistant turned Elvis impersonator — and that is all he was, no matter how heatedly he denied it — and a therapist who is seeing men in nightclubs without even discussing it with her long-term patients first, and the love of my life who is two-timing me with another man without even knowing it, and my best friend, who is moving in on the one man from my past who could make me forget that man who is two-timing me and bringing me enough pain to sue for punitive damages.

Throw in Fauna, and you've got *This Is Your Life*.

Now, ordinarily in these situations I only do one thing — pout. And I don't know whether it was by her scraping at my inner thigh with her massive nails, or by her muttering at me in what I thought was German, but Thallassa's presence drove me to action.

First I tried the amazed and utterly charmed approach, in which you wave one hand in a circular motion from the wrist as you mouth broadly, "Hey, come here," with a look of discovery on your face. As if you've just opened King Tut's tomb.

When that didn't work, mostly due to the fact that neither Pixie or Orly were looking anywhere in my direction, I got up and went over there, the long way, around the edges of the room, behind pillars.

As I passed by Dina's table, I could swear that she looked as if she were not happy. Not truly. Forget the champagne or the fact that she was wearing red, a color I didn't think she'd ever even acknowledged, much less purchased. The woman looked ten years older. As if she'd lost her best friend.

As I passed by Thor and his pet pig they leaned toward one another to whisper, until their foreheads nearly touched. "You're leaning toward the wrong face," I thought again and again. "You are. You are."

By the time I got to Orly's table, I'd ripped off my Happy New Year hat. Who needed this shit anyway? Maybe I'd just go back to the other table, wait for midnight, and then kiss Thallassa. And I might have, too, except she looked as if she kissed with her teeth.

And also because Pixie, seeing me lurking overhead with indecision, reached up and took my hand and brought it down to the table top and reintroduced into my life the man named Orly Kasaba.

He reached over to my hand on the tabletop, a look of vague recognition in his eyes. I took his warm, firm hand in mine to shake it. I had no intention of ever letting go.

20

January 7

Dear Diary,

So, I spent the entire morning in front of the mirror, worrying what to wear to lunch with Orly. Even if it had taken me the better part of two hours of pure charm on New Year's Eve to get the lunch date. And even if I had had to fight my urge to grab and kiss him at midnight to be sure of his keeping the lunch date. And even if — and this was the hard part — I had had to watch while Pixie did kiss him at midnight, right after Benny had finished singing "My Way" and ascending to heaven on an almost invisible wire to become the King Angel, the seventh age of Elvis. She just took his thickly bearded face in her hands and drew his lips first toward and then onto her own.

For my part, discretion forced my eyes away from Pixie and Orly and off around the room. Thallassa netted a passing waiter and used him as the object of a New Year's spree. Dina and companion kissed, not with rapture, but with affection. And Thor and his pig-dog gazed into each other's eyes, their hands all busy busy busy under the table.

I rose to the occasion and to my feet, hefting Orly's flagon of champagne and calling Happy New Year. Everyone turned in my direction. Some with recognition, some without, but a good time was had by all.

Now, some days later, having had two distinctly pleasant telephone conversations with Orly, he and I are meeting for lunch.

Within the confines of the conversations, I managed to learn that Orly now is director and C.E.O of Kasaba Brothers, a chain of men's clothing stores. Just the thought of there being more at home like this one is enough to curl your hair.

I also got his address under pretense of thank-you notes, something no one, other than my mother, has written for twenty years. It is in one of those white white raised slab monstrosities that have revitalized the city's core. One can only imagine the oversized vases filled with dried branches that must inhabit such a space. And a fireplace with glass wall screen. And wall-to-wall carpets in some pastel shade, with trim in salmon and grey.

Oh, Orly, Orly, Orly, I'm going to have to take you in hand.

So we meet for lunch at the restaurant of his choosing. It has a raw bar, which I take to be possibly a very good sign. And what does he do but spend the next hour pumping me for information about our dear Pixie. Is she available? Has she had many past lovers? And the usual Arab/French question: Can she cook?

I answer with sweetness and honesty as Pixie is the finest of the fine. Too fine for this hairy macho jerkoff who is, as far as I can tell, just about perfect for me.

I decide to get him drunk.

Which just wasn't hard to do, as he had been doing his best to help me for the better part of an hour. Well, anyway, I had the chance to say to the waiter something I've always wanted to say, as I waved a ten in his face and said, "Keep 'em coming." And Orly kept them going, too.

Soon, his pasta salad nearly untouched, the table is laden

with empties. Of all sorts of drinks. And Orly has moved from sparkle eyes to red-faced to slurring his words something fierce. I, of course, have been watering the potted palm with my liquor.

Step one, I figure, and then move on to step two. We leave my battered Datsun in its parking place when finally the check has been taken care of, and we get into his little BMW. I drive. To his place. I just had to see if my guesses were correct.

Which, of course, they were. And more so. No black velvet paintings, but everything up to that point. The sort of art that matches the sofa. That you get at hotel/motel art shows where the canvases are priced by size.

Blue was his pastel color, with the salmon and gray trim. The glass-front fireplace was of the sort that stand in the middle of the room, opening into both the living area and the kitchen. And the kitchen had a white tile floor. The fact that it was still clean meant either there was a cleaning woman or the room had never been used. I guessed the second possibility, as the rest of the apartment looked as if it had been under bombardment.

There was something so utterly male about the place. About the underwear that I saw on the floor of the bedroom when I helped Orly stagger to his bed.

All he did was moan when I tossed him on his bed. I then watched him float about on a sea of nausea as the waterbed rippled. Served him right for owning such a thing. He moaned again as I pulled off his shoes.

"Let me help you get comfy," I said, and pulled away his socks. He lay with one arm across his face, still bouncing slightly up and down on the shivering bed.

I then helped him get more comfy by unbuttoning the buttons of his shirt, starting with the sleeve that lay across his eyes. Slowly, I worked with the buttons down his chest. With the opening of each new space, I saw more and more

of the broad and very densely forested expanse of his chest.
I saw the torso of an ex-football player who had only slightly
let himself go to pot. The pecs were still there, with their
nipples standing erect, and the navel was only slightly deeper
from the inclusion of a little fat.

Softly and sweetly, I pulled his shirt from his pants,
letting my hands accidently flow across his stomach as I did
so. Again he moaned, I thought perhaps with less pain this
time.

And then I had to face my moment of truth. Should I
believe that he was now comfortable enough and get the
hell out of here? Or should I realize, as a friend, that Orly
would be ever so much more comfortable if I helped him
out of his pants?

I paused for a moment, but only for a moment. And
then I reached for the button to those pants.

It opened abruptly, with the button flying off across
the room to ping to the floor in the corner. Perhaps I am
a little overeager, I told myself. I looked up at Orly, who
now lay with both hands covering his face, as if in prayer.
No news was good news, I figured, and moved on to the fly.

I unzipped his trousers slowly, savoring the moment.
Would that I had had the gall to do it with my teeth. Under
the soft fabric, I managed to feel the soft lump of his
genitalia, all asleep in their little bed.

The pants unzipped, I moved down to the foot of the
bed and to Orly's ankles and stood ready to help his pants
in their long journey down to the floor. I looked up again
toward his face, and, from beneath his hands, felt sure that
I could hear the sound of soft breathing.

It took me five minutes, I'm sure, to get those pants off
those wonderful muscular legs without disturbing the goods.
But I did, and he lay very very still, as if waiting to see what
would happen next.

I have to admit I wondered myself.

Here's the situation I faced: I was standing above the almost nude figure of the man I have lusted after since college. If I were truly interested in a relationship with this person, I doubt that I would have gone for the "I was so drunk I didn't know what I was doing" motif. But perhaps his obvious and obviously reciprocated interest in Pixie frightened me into quick action, so that things between them would not have progressed far enough for me not to be able to feign ignorance when Pixie looked at me with accusation in her eyes.

And yet, here I stood. Without a moment's thought about Thor. After all, Orly predated Thor. Right? And that gave him certain rights and me certain rights too, to enjoy the possibilities inherent in what I knew — from the shower room — of Orly's complex and mature build.

And yet, here, too, was a man who had given me no signal as to his desire of me. And who could break me in two with just his forearm.

And yet, if I was not very very mistaken, here was a man who was getting a visible erection in his Perry Ellis underwear. Perhaps because, while I mused and wondered at the possibilities of this moment, I teased the tip of his penis, drawing little circles on top of the lump within the blue bikini briefs.

As the pink tip began to push itself out of the briefs, I edged the elastic back just a bit for a better view.

There was the little face of the cock, the slit like a mouth, the head large and red.

I pulled the elastic lower, to see the vein throbbing and the penis pulsing gently. All within a nest of deep rich black hair.

I traced the vein softly with the tip of my finger. And lowered the briefs the rest of the way. There were his balls, as if he'd taken them from a horse, huge dense hairy sacs. The secret of his success.

I touched them softly with my fingers. Brushed his hair softly with my hands. And then, knowing I was a better man for waiting for the invitation that I also knew would never come, I slowly moved the briefs back into position. And walked to the bedroom door.

I wish I could say now that I just tiptoed out the door and gave the man over to Pixie to do with as she pleased, but this would not be true.

In truth, I walked to the bedroom door and then turned back. Such opportunities don't come often.

Again, I lowered those tight-fitting briefs. Again, his organ sprang into action. Only this time, while still doing my best not to disturb the man, I gave his best friend a very friendly welcome.

Orly's hips moved in the right rhythm. His breathing grew more rapid. And, again he turned to moaning.

And then it was all over and well worth it.

Perhaps I can do the right thing and just leave this man for Pixie, my best friend, who so desperately needs a good relationship to get her away from her married man. But perhaps not. For what is often said about a dog who has tasted blood can now be said for me, as I have tasted Orly. . . .

21

Stardate 2103/13
Dear Dream Diary,
   I find myself standing in the living room of an old house. There is no furniture and only the tattered rags of old lace curtains on the windows. Light beams slant down from the outside, with dust motes racing up and down the beams. The hard wood beneath my feet is stained and drab.
   I walk throughout the house. Each impression is very detailed. Light, shadow, dark.
   There is a long, high curved stairway. I try to see what is at the top, but I cannot. Something inside me tells me that I must climb to the top.
   And I do, I begin to climb, although the effort is great. I am a salmon struggling upstream. One step at a time, my feet heavy as lead, my legs aching.
   Suddenly, from the top of the stairs, I hear the sounds of a hammer pounding, the cutting edge of a saw working.
   And then there is the sound of a voice. "These baseboards will have to go, of course." It says, "At the time this house was built, the boards were often installed before the floor coverings, making them hard to remove, but in this case, they're just nailed right on, making it easy to pull them right back off again, there."
   And, as I reach the top of the stairs. I see a man with a beard pulling off the baseboards with the help of a crowbar. The mans calls me Norm. He begins to fire questions at me as to the condition of the wood in the house, whether or not support beams will have to be replaced.

I want to tell the man that I am not Norm. That I do not understand what he wants from me. But I look down at my body, see the huge belly, see the tool belt, work boots, and coveralls and I know that I am Norm, but that I have somehow forgotten everything I used to know about the restoration of old houses.

There is sawdust everywhere, it forms a fog on the inside of the house. I want to cry out, to run away, but my body works with a will of its own. I find myself sawing wood, hammering boards in place. Something in me knows what it's doing. Something in me wants to restore this old house.

But inside me is a portion that is not Norm. That wants to be younger and finer, that wants no part of sawdust.

I call the bearded man by name. I tell him that everything will be ready in three days, if there is no rain.

Every time I turn around we are in a new place, another part of the house. One moment I am hammering, the next, sawing. Always apparently knowing just what I'm doing and doing just what I most love doing.

And yet, I am not and I do not. Part of me wants more than anything else to burst out of this body I've made. To cry out, "I'm not Norm, not Norm, not Norm. . . ."

And then I wake up as I always wake up — screaming.

22

For the first two years or so, I could always lie to Dina. Until she had heard enough of my life to put two and two together. Until I grew confused as to how I had explained what to her. Like whether or not I said I went to the Junior Prom and with whom I said that I had gone. Anyway, there was a honeymoon period in which she at least seemed to believe anything I told her, when she seemed to be on my side.

Not so with Fauna. She catches me at falsehoods before I can even speak them. It's getting a little eerie, how she just takes my hand for a second, after she's given me my cranberry juice, and then laces into me.

You should have heard her on the subject of Orly Kasaba. How I was not his karmic mate, Pixie was, and how dare I get involved. She insists, however, that Orly has no memory of the event and that, in his reality, it never took place, so, if I just keep my mouth shut — in more ways than one, no doubt — it will be better for everyone.

I don't think she likes me.

And I'm not sure I like her, either, or if anyone should be a psychic and a counselor. Why can't she just tell me what horse is going to win in the sixth race tomorrow and let it go at that, instead of playing omniscient or something like it?

So I go there every Tuesday, and it's not even covered by my medical plan at work, so it's an extra fifty dollars a week out of my pocket for her to scream at me and call it psychic guidance.

"You are going to have a change of scenery," she told me last week. I could have told her that, what with the holidays over and the white sales beginning. Suddenly, it's sheets, sheets, sheets and there are only so many ways you can take those stubby little display beds they give you and make them look exciting — sexy, even. Besides, this year's sheets are mostly Laura Ashley clones, with dimity little floral designs and vomitous colors.

Or maybe it's just me.

Or maybe it's that Benny had Thallassa call me to say that he'd left on his world tour, without even bothering to come by the store and say that he didn't want to work with me again. I mean, I always knew that it was a temporary sort of thing for Benny to be doing. Just until his muse struck, as he would put it, until he got the idea for his next show, but he HAD, at one time, really wanted the job, after all. And he HAD gone around with a measuring tape around his neck looking quite content for weeks and weeks — much longer that anyone would have thought.

And now he was gone. Like he'd never been there, like he'd keeled over from some terminal disease. Without a good-bye.

And this made me sullen, I must admit. Because with the secret guilt I had toward Pixie, that I'd slept with her new boyfriend before she'd had a chance to, just as I'd slept with her brother over and over without her ever knowing, well, it was getting in the way of my friendship with her. I suddenly didn't want to talk to her and wouldn't pick up the telephone answering machine when I heard her voice, as I always used to. I just didn't know what to say to her, how to explain, except to use the classic, "I saw him first," which never seems to work with this sort of thing.

So, with Benny suddenly gone and Pixie being kept at the necessary distance, it left me pretty low and lonely.

Lonely enough that I'd finally gone to the Sweat It Out class that Benny and I were always supposed to go to.

And there, of course, I saw Randy, the pig-dog, and the bald man who stood behind Benny whenever toe-touching time came around.

The woman who runs the class, Arlene, is one of those blonde women who have abdomens that seem to have been carved from wood, and who wear hot pink and black in leotard combinations.

She runs the class like a tight ship. With a whistle around her neck, a sweatband on her forehead and little weights on her arms and legs.

The class meets in the basement of a church and is comprised of myself, the other two aforementioned gentlemen, and about fifteen ladies.

As it was my first class, I got to take it for free.

We started by warming up our arms and legs to the music of the Rolling Stones. After that, Talking Heads got our blood rushing to our heads as we pulled weeds and touched our toes. At this point, I was somewhat amused to notice that the bald man, who began the class standing behind Randy, moved to stand behind me. Luckily, I had decided not to wear shorts, but instead covered my body in a loose sweat suit.

Then came some loud and crashing music that I did not recognize, and everyone began to run around the room in a clockwise fashion. This gave me my first chance to greet Randy as we ran in a joint formation. I nodded in his direction, and he greeted me with the very words that I would have staked my life would be his first, "How's it going?"

I ran with him for as long as I could and then watched him pull ahead and hurry off, as did the bald man and fourteen of the fifteen women. The only other person who remained at my pace could have given birth to my mother.

Obviously, sweat it out I did.

As the class was in a church, the shower facilities were smaller and more makeshift than at a regular health club. In fact, the shower room was little larger than a single stall. Which gave me ample opportunity to watch Randy in the buff. To view the enemy, to catch him unaware. Just let him drop his soap, I prayed.

And yet, as the warm water rushed over my aching body, I began to feel a kindness grow within me toward Randy. In the first place, it was not his fault that he stood between me and Thor. After all, he didn't even know that I knew, that I had a habit of following strange men and watching them kiss other men in parking garages. And he might even have true and real and deep feelings for Thor, not that I didn't have potentially realer and truer and deeper feelings of my own, unless, of course, things had a chance of working out between me and Orly, in which case Randy could just keep Thor with my blessings.

But I had to admit I doubted then and still do that anyone named that worst of all names — Randy — could have real or true or deep feelings about anything. But still I was trying to give him the benefit of the doubt.

And the second reason for the benefit of the doubt was that he seemed to be a regular guy. An OK Joe. The white boy's white boy. He looked like his skin was the type that never tanned right, that just burned, what with his brown hair and real light light blue eyes. One of those true fair-haired boys. He just reeked of offices and pin-striped suits. But he was trying hard to be an OK Joe, what with "How's it going?" and all.

But there was a third reason why I was beginning to rethink my opinion of old Randy, a reason Benny should have told me but didn't, probably because he was afraid it would have upset me terribly if he had told me, which it would have, by making me feel inadequate. But, now

seeing it and discovering it for myself, I had to admit it was
really not a bad thing, in fact it was pretty great.

See, Randy had a cock that hung nearly to his knees.

I've never seen anything like it before. And given the
cellulite that he really really did have and his kind of flat
ass, not to mention his skin and his lack of stirring intellect,
it gave me a pretty good understanding of how he had
landed a guy like Thor in the first place.

All of which made me not hate the old pig-dog as much
as I used to. After all, what chance did that rocket launcher
of a cock have against me with my arms akimbo?

Which brings me back to Fauna. And the differences
between Dina and Fauna. The first of which being that I used
to feel that I could tell Dina anything. And she would react
with the same wide-eyed innocence that she'd used to react
to everything else I'd already told her. But with Fauna, I have
the feeling that there's no reason to tell her anything. No
point, really. Because she seems to either already know
something psychically, or not be interested in knowing it
at all.

She seems to be the one who does all the talking. So
I don't get to mention Pixie or Orly or Randy or anyone.
I just sit with my hands folded around my glass of cranberry
juice — and here is another vital difference between the two,
as I very much prefer my herbal tea to my cranberry juice —
and listen to what she has to say.

Today she pretty much has decided that she has solved
my two great needs with just one person. My need for a new
friend to replace Benny and Dina who have betrayed me
hatefully and Pixie who I hatefully betrayed. And my need
for help at work, since all my assistants have betrayed me
and left me in the dust.

It seems that Fauna has a friend who needs a friend and

a job — in that order, Fauna insists. And who is perfect for all my needs, most especially in that she is a she and is therefore not going to contribute in any way to my already overly complicated life style.

I immediately agreed to meet with and most likely hire this woman, in that I recognize that I do indeed need both a friend and an assistant, in that I feel as if I've hit the wall of creativity in terms of white sales and sheets. But I begin to feel just a little apprehensive when Fauna tells me that this woman's name is Mantis.

23

So when I meet Mantis bright and early the next morning, my first emotion is fear. Then humor, then sorrow.

I mean, if anyone ever was well-named. . .well, let me set the whole thing up.

I'm arranging sheets, what else, into sort of miasmic swirls of pastel and Laura Ashley-ish vomitous color and design, when suddenly by my side a small women is standing. I neither hear nor see her arrive. But there she is, dressed in the sort of jumpsuit that the Dragon Lady would wear if the Dragon Lady ever wore a jumpsuit. All black and skin-tight with a Nehru jacket collar. The overall effect is like a priest's skin-diving vestments.

"Mantis," she says, with the slightest suggestion of a bow. Not, "Hi there, I'm Mantis," or "My name is Mantis, how do you do?" or anything that a human might say. Just "Mantis."

So we left the floor and went back to my office. Even by this time, with her just having said the one word, I knew that I'd done it again in terms of hiring another mistake — all my assistants seem to be either mentally challenged or Fiends from Hell.

As we walked and I stepped back to allow her to enter the doorway to my office first, I noticed that from her thick black leather belt hung a power stapler. I noticed also that the brooch that was pinned across her throat was made up of cast-off bits of metal — staples, bobby pins, paper clips, and the like — that had been glued together in this sort of mass and then covered with glitter.

But it wasn't until she began to speak a little to tell me about her training as an Underground Designer — sort of a Keith Haring kind of riff in which Mantis went about making New York subway platforms into living rooms, dining rooms, and bedrooms — that I began to notice that something was fishy with the Dragon Lady.

It was the accent. More Texas than Tokyo. Better she should stick to monosyllables.

And when you got a good look at her eyes and saw that it was the kohl outlines and not the natural centers that gave them their slant, well, then the whole thing suddenly seemed normal and typical and you knew that my new assistant was just mentally challenged as usual rather than a Fiend from Hell.

So I looked at her portfolio, a collection of shots of furniture and brick-a-brac tossed about on subway platforms and pretended to be excited by her work. I told her that the job was hers. Although why I did such a thing I will never, ever know, other than the fact that I suspected that the quality of my session with Fauna depended upon my doing as I was told and hiring this Mantis person as my new assistant.

Perhaps it was some karmic thing, that I could skip

fifty years in purgatory for hiring someone I'd stepped on in a previous life, or maybe it was more basic — that Fauna had the neurotic need to control everyone and everything in her path. (I don't know this for a fact, I only know that Dina always used to listen to me talk and then ask questions like, "How does that make you feel?" or "What are you going to do about that?" and that Fauna doesn't even let me talk because she says that she already knows what I'm going to say and that if I just listen to her, I can get the most for my money, as I can only afford an hour a week.)

So I hire this woman, give her a tape measure — which she hangs off her belt like the power stapler — and send her out to deal with sheets sheets sheets.

The sorrow part of my three-part rain of emotion is this: suddenly, as I sat back in my design office, with dried and silk flowers all around me like on the gravestones at Flanders Field, it seemed suddenly that my life was no longer my own. That bits of my life with names like Benny and Pixie were flying off into other places and leaving me behind, for if Benny was my right hand, then Pixie surely was my heart. Not to mention Dina being my brain. Which left this body, this person a little tattered and a little hollow. I felt like a tumbleweed in the wind, like someone watching the *Titanic* go down, like a child trapped on a roller coaster, on which the first ride was great fun, the second and third just fine, the fourth through seventh scary and now, at the twentieth or more, a terrifying combination.

Little did I know as I sat back in that room, twirling my tape measure around my middle finger and feeling muy muy sorry for myself, that the roller coaster ride was really just beginning. And that, out on the sales floor, Mantis was creating a sensation in fitted sheets, finding more positions for them than the Kama Sutra had sex acts.

This would have been my moment of decision, my moment for pulling the turnip out of the fertile ground of

Tara and declaring that I would never go hungry again. But I did not yet know that I possibly could go hungry. I did not know that a decision would have to be made.

I only knew that I would have to hurry if I was to make the noontime exercise class at Arlene's.

24

Stardate 2146/74
Dear Dream Diary,

Dreamed I was Norm again. This time we worked on converting an old barn. I spent weeks on the roof, shingling.

I still do not know the meaning of these dreams, but I am beginning to enjoy my work and find comfort in the restoration of old things, old houses.

Perhaps we can work by the ocean next. I would like that. Maybe one of those old houses up at Cape Cod?

25

I really don't know why I answered the telephone, instead of just letting the answering machine pick it up. But there I was with freshly laundered sheets, all nice and folded, en route to the linen closet, when as I passed the telephone, it rang.

Of course, on the other end of it was Pixie, who was all in wonder and out of breath at having caught me at home, instead of the machine that has been protecting me from her calls for the last few days since my lunch with Orly.

"Where have you been?" she asked. "Why haven't you returned my calls?"

I told her that I was busy breaking in a new assistant at work and managed to turn the conversation around to a list of Mantis' foibles and get Pixie away from the subject of me and Orly.

Then she said, "Orly wanted me to apologize to you for drinking so much the other day. He wanted me to thank you for getting him home safely."

Now, not for one moment did I actually believe that I was getting away with the events of the Day of the Lunch, but Pixie seemed to want to just not explore the subject until she continued, "And I wanted you to have dinner with Orly and me at my place on Thursday."

Then I knew we were playing the spider and the fly. And yet, I said yes to the invitation.

Now, one might ask why one would say yes to an

invitation to dine with your best friend and her new boyfriend, with whom only days before you had had a sexual experience, albeit one that he seems not to remember. Well, the reasons are twofold.

First, I figure that if Fauna is correct about any of the things she repeatedly bleats at me, then there just might be something to this karma rationale. And I might as well take my lumps for my little failings in this life and not have to worry about them in the next. In other words, the worry about all this is just too draining and I just want to get the damned thing over with.

But there is a second reason, and it is not one that can be easily dismissed. Call me crazy, but I have a real problem with turning down a free meal — any free meal anywhere at any time. I mean, if Hitler had invited me to dinner, I might not have accepted, there are limits to everything, but, then again, I might have said all right, but I had to be home early.

I mean, I've never really gotten into the subject of money, but, even if I talk about it more, sex is of no greater importance to me than is money. It's just that, given my job, I get a little money on a lot more regular basis than I do sex. That might be why I fixate more on the one.

But never forget that my mother's major life policy is "When it's gone, it's gone." And although that carried right through sex and love, it mostly foisted itself on the rest of us in terms of money. And still today, I lay out my little pile of money that is mine to spend each week — my allowance for myself, if you will — and when that's gone, it's gone and there's no more money until next week.

Now, this may sound a little odd, but remember, my work is retail. The one great asset of working retail is that you get paid each and every week. Every Wednesday. The one big drawback is that you get paid so very little every week.

Which leaves me driving a battered Datsun — and what

did they make these cars out of anyway, some special metal
that was created to rust and rot away? — while Orly Kasaba
drives a BMW.

Not that I'm complaining, but remember, I get paid on
Wednesdays and have to somehow keep hold of enough
money to pay Fauna the next Tuesday evening. And that's
a lot of lunches in between.

Besides, Pixie's really a good good little cook, to answer
Orly's typical European male question about her.

So, anyway, I'm sort of approaching Thursday evening as
a lemming does a cliff. And, in the meantime, I've got other
things to worry about.

The first is Mantis, who, in just the few days that she's
worked for me, has straightened out completely our design
office. All my pens are stacked neatly in a coffee mug. All
the papers are stacked by size. All the dried and silk flowers
have been placed in bins by color.

And, to make matters worse, she is doing her level best
to get along with everyone. Except me. I still can never see
or hear her coming. She is suddenly just there, by my side,
with some new design idea or display function.

And, although I cannot prove it, I swear she is living
in the store. She arrives before me, no matter how early I
try and get to work. And she goes home after me, no
matter how late I stay. If I suggest that she leave, she just
tells me that there's a little work she wants to finish up and
then she'll be on her way. But that little bit of work always
manages to last until I've given up arranging my pens within
their coffee mug and have just gone home for the day.

But, worst of all, this Mantis person has a way of refer-
ring to herself in the third person. Instead of saying "me"
she says "this one." As in, "This one would like to go to
lunch now." And she says it while casting her gaze at the

floor or at the toes that she curls under within her little ballet shoes.

I mean talk about karma, what did I ever do to the universe that I have to end up with every freak of nature as my assistant? Is there some cosmic law that says only feebs and Nazis should apply?

And, to make matters worse, there's the little event that happened to me today at Arlene's Sweat It Out.

I had taken the class as I've been doing say three or four times a week and I was very pleased to find that I was at last able to pass that grandmother as we ran our laps. Meaning that in just these last few days I have moved up from last to next to last, which is something at least.

And then we did our floor exercises, and it was not until we were touching our toes that I noticed that the bald guy was missing. So I finished class, figuring that it really wasn't that important, it's just that I've kind of gotten used to him positioning himself right behind my rump. Like it's my last little grasp at youth or something.

But then, as I was walking back to the locker room, I realized that this means Randy and I will have the place all to ourselves. And, for a moment, I was kind of sorry that there was no way I could get him quickly drunk at the health club. But the moment passed and I just kind of undressed and walked into the shower, where Randy was already busily soaping his privates and humming a songless tune.

And I have to kind of admit that, for a moment there, I could see what Thor saw in Randy. He was sort of a large puppy of a man. All arms and legs. Sort of in shape but sort of not. The kind of body that, even if it were ever in the best shape it could possibly be in, would not be anything to get carried away over. I mean, he's just sort of so flesh-toned, all over.

But there he was, washing his belly in that happy way that reduces all men to boys. And I looked him over top to bottom and stem to stern, as he turned his body toward me and away from the water. He's got the kind of torso that would have love handles no matter how thin the rest of him got. And he has one little patch of hair over his solar plexus, although the rest of his chest is smooth. And those little pin-point nipples that almost don't exist at all.

And he's got those real real hairy legs and a hairy butt and a generous pubic zone, with a little rope of hair extending up to his navel.

And I don't know whether or not he could feel my eyes darting all over him, I mean, I always thought I was better at the game than to let my interest show, but suddenly he started talking to me. About little things. About class and exercise and how it's important to work at keeping in shape when you're getting near thirty. I figured that he was giving me the benefit of the doubt here and agreed loudly.

And then, after the water had been turned off, leaving a sudden sense of quiet, he said to me, "We should get together for lunch after the noontime class sometime."

I agreed that we should.

"Well, how about Friday?" he asked.

And damned if free food didn't win again.

All of which has me jumpy. Has me worried. The boyfriend of my next boyfriend. The boyfriend of my best friend. So I had drunken sex with one and want to bear children for the other. Why shouldn't I have my meals with their true loves. After all, am I not the ultimate Hound of Hell?

26

The dinner started out just fine, it really did.

It wasn't until later that things took a turn for the worse.

In retrospect, I can't believe that I made the same mistake that Orly Kasaba had made so recently at lunch. Only I made it with gin.

I had had a couple after work and before going to Pixie's. In fact, the sheer anxiety that I felt in terms of this dinner had made me more or less worthless the entire day. In fact, I spent the entire afternoon in the store's beauty salon, getting my hair subtly highlighted with sort of a golden color. I also had the chance to listen while the boys in the salon bitched to and about each other, something that usually picks me right up, by letting me see that there are those with lives more complicated than my own. I never enter the salon without hearing about whose lover ran off with whom; and who wrapped their new Corvette, bought with the insurance money from their last car (the one that was stolen outside a gay bar,) into what tree right outside who's door.

I went to get my hair fixed, as I've already noted, out of sheer anxiety. I find it calming. Plus the boys at the salon always work me in at a moment's notice and never charge me. And if there is something akin to a free meal, it is a free haircut.

But I also went because I've given up on trying to keep up with our control Mantis. Her displays have subtlety and subtext that simply paralyze me. In fact, they are inscrutable. That is the word. I can no longer bear to watch her at work. The gaffers tape seems to do her bidding. Displays just seem to flow from her fingertips.

So I'm in the beauty salon, trying to walk a delicate line with Tommy, who is doing me. I mean, if I am rude to him and refuse to flirt when flirted with, he might actually charge me for this afternoon of beauty, right? And, if I flirt too well, I could end up in all sorts of trouble. I mean, Tommy has slept with everything that lies down, no matter where.

So I regale him with tales of exercise class and of the bald man, who I refer to as being "hot." I don't mention that he is bald, but later think that I should have, in that Tommy would be sure in a relationship with this guy that he was not being loved for his hair-care skills. To hear him tell it, he has been loved and lost in the past for his skill with scissors.

Anyway, by the time I am out of the chair, I figure that I might as well go on out and give myself the rest of the day off.

Only, as can happen, I no sooner get out of the door than I didn't know what to do with myself for the three hours until I was due at Pixie's. So I went to a pay phone and called Fauna, to see if she could work me in. But I got her answering machine, which features what seems like four or five minutes of unconstructed New Age music before getting the beep, so I hung up.

Then, I have to admit, I called Dina's answering machine. Not to leave a message. Just to hear her voice.

So, by the time it came time for dinner, I had had a few gins and tonics in an anonymous bar.

And there, when Pixie opened the door, all pert and

perky in a pink dress, sat Orly Kasaba, all Vlad-the-Impaler gorgeous, right there on the Naugahyde couch.

Pixie and I just sat quietly for a few moments, just drinking in his looks. Then we all had drinks. More gin for me.

Now, I thought that things were going pretty well, although Pixie and Orly did seem to be glancing in each other's direction a good bit, out of lust or worry over my behavior, I could not be sure.

But we made it into dinner and sat slicing our chicken and making small talk. I had begun to notice that there were patches of quiet in the evening. Moments in which everyone seemed too embarrassed to speak. Still, I could not be sure why the two of them seemed embarrassed. I only knew why I was.

And the moments of quiet grew in length and depth until the conversation was what was happening in patches. And then the only sound was chewing. Chewing, chewing, chewing. I thought I would go mad.

It was a *film noir* moment. I was in a giant spider's web and I could hear the spider chewing and chewing and chewing.

Suddenly I spoke. I heard myself speak — or scream, really.

"I slept with your brother," I screamed. I shrieked.

The words just came out of my mouth. They came out unbidden. They just poured out, good and loud.

And then I looked at Pixie. She actually said "EEK!" like women in cartoons do when confronted with a live mouse. But she didn't jump on the chair, she ran from the room crying loudly.

And then Orly Kasaba was everywhere. His face was as huge as the moon, hanging over me.

And he punched me good and hard in the mouth. I didn't actually feel the blow, thanks to the gin buffer, but

I acknowledged its power by spitting out a tooth. I felt the pain the next morning.

"Just get out, get out, get out!" Pixie screamed from the other room. Obviously I'd touched a nerve, either of Pixie's memory of our childhood together — herself, myself, and her brother — or she had some suspicions as to Orly. And I didn't know why I'd blurted out something that I'd kept secret for over a decade, except it seemed better to deal with a potentially harmless memory than to confess to a more recent crime, and I was sure that I was not going to get out of that dinner without paying for something.

So I picked up my tooth and left.

The next day, I called in sick at work and rolled back over in bed to moan and groan until it was time for Arlene. It seemed like a way to work out the toxins in my system, or, at least, another way of punishing myself.

Besides, I'd worked myself up to a frazzle over my lunch with Randy, and there was no way I was going to miss it.

Over lunch, at a not nice, not bad restaurant, Randy could not help notice my bizarre method of chewing. So I unwrapped my handkerchief and showed him the tooth. And told him something about how some display had toppled and hit me on the head.

He gave me an aspirin out of what looked like a lizard-skin pill holder and then said, "Hey, I have the best dentist. And he's right in the same mall you work in. Let me give you his name."

He took out one of his business cards and wrote on the back, Lawrence Papsun, D.D.S., and the doctor's phone number.

I'm beginning to think that I was wrong about this guy Randy.

27

I CAN'T BELIEVE IT!
THOR'S A DENTIST!
HE'S A FUCKING NAZI DENTIST AND I JUST WANT
TO DIE!!!!!!!!!!!!!!!!!!!

28

Shock follows shock.

I mean. . . .

I mean, there I was, already in pain. I wander into the dentist's office, having called to make an emergency appointment, and I just walk right in the door, thinking that it is so convenient to my work, being in the medical wing of the mall and all, and how I'm sure that my medical plan will cover this and that the dentist's nurse should give me no problem with being billed since I'm just downstairs every day and all. And I sit there like a good boy and read a copy of *Newsweek* that is so old that it has Jim and Tammie Bakker on the cover. And then the nurse calls my name and I get up and follow her down the hall and into a chamber of horrors that is the dentist's office. And she seats me in the dentist's chair, which is high and curved and almost enveloping. And the chair faces a super-graphic of the moon that fills an entire wall of the office. So I'm just sitting there looking at the moon in greater detail than I have ever seen it before and I'm nervous enough because I HATE dentists. And I didn't need to see *Marathon Man* to form that opinion. So I'm just sitting there contemplating the moon and whether or not I can live the rest of my life without this tooth that came from somewhere in the middle of the top row of the left side of my mouth. I think it's one of the food grinders, it isn't one of the food mashers or rippers. And my mind is going like this, a mile a minute, half thinking that the pain I've already gone through and will not go through here in this office is nothing less than I truly truly deserve because I have caused great pain to Pixie, who has done me no wrong. And things are going along this way, and I've just about decided to stuff cotton balls into the tooth gap and just get the hell out of here, when a low, rumbly voice says, "Hello," and my chair gets turned around to face the dental equipment. And the voice, while I'm turning, says, "I always like to let everyone get a good look at the moon instead of the drills." And there is a throaty little laugh. And I'm scared enough to die by now anyway and so I look at the dentist and IT IS THOR AND THOR IS LAWRENCE PAPSUN, D.D.S. And it is a dentist who shamelessly kissed that pig-dog Randy — I don't care how big his dick is — in the back of the car on a hot hot summer night and ruined my life. And then I looked at his hands and they were clean, oh, so clean, so painfully clean and I knew. I knew that he'd been a dentist all along and that he'd been trying to tell me he was a dentist, with his high hairline and his blue-gray eyes and his clean clean hands and his sans-a-belt trousers. And I looked into his eyes again and I didn't care that he was a dentist. Not even a clean clean

Nazi dentist. Because of his blue-gray eyes. Not even when he said, "Well, well now," as he unwrapped my little tooth from the cloth I'd carried it into the office in. Not even when he said, "This will hurt a little." And then I knew, I knew that the Novocain was working because my head was swimming and everything went blue-gray and then black. And then I knew. . .I knew. . .And he put his hands into my mouth and I was helpless before him and he was causing me pain. Pain. Which was just as it should have been. Pain. Distant aching pain that would come later, from its distance and sit on my jaw. And I knew the irony that this man that I'd loved, that I had worshipped from afar, would invade my body with his hands and would cause me pain. And again I forgave Randy and hoped he would forgive me as I stood before the future prostrate naked Lawrence Papsun, D.D.S., with my arms akimbo and said, "Come, put your hands inside me and make me ache." And there was floating and there was noise and drilling and the world turned orange and then it turned red and I knew. . .I knew the irony of the universe that Orly Kasaba would hit me, not for what I'd done to him, but what I'd done to Pixie and done ten years ago, and that that blow would send me to the pig-dog whore-faced Randy, who, out of kindness, would send me here and to this man, to Lawrence Papsun, D.D.S., who seemed hell-bent to drill a hole in the side of my face. And on and on it went. I never stopped to breathe. He never once said, "Spit." I knew, I knew, I just knew when it was time to. And round and round the world went, and I wanted, so wanted to see the moon again. To be weightless in his arms and float high about a Speilberg full moon. And never, never float back down. . . .

As I say, shock followed shock.

29

Given that this is Saturday morning, I am in bed watching *Pee Wee's Playhouse*. Even though it is one of those episodes featuring Cowboy Curtis — with whom I believe Pee Wee shares a special friendship — I cannot help but be sad.

For one thing, they never should have redecorated the Playhouse. It was perfect in the show's first year. And, personally, I very much miss Mrs. Steve and Globie's old face. Not to mention Trixie and the old and real and true King of Cartoons. Do the producers think that all black men look alike and no one will notice that they've changed Kings?

And then there is Captain Carl. How could they have dropped him from the show? I keep on telling myself that he left under his own power, going on to better things, but I never see him on any other show, not even on commercials, so I'm pretty much convinced that they gave him the old heave-ho. But I always thought that Captain Carl would end up with Miss Yvonne. I guess it just wasn't to be.

And Jambi's not even on the show enough anymore. Only Terry remains from the group of my favorites.

Well, these were the things that went through my head as I sat watching the television. These and other thoughts, like: "I wonder how Pixie is and if she'll ever speak to me again in this lifetime?" and "I wonder what I can possibly do to get Lawrence Papsun, D.D.S., in bed?"

There were moments of bliss in the dentist's chair.

Especially those moments when the dentist rubs up against you as he is working on your teeth. When his thigh presses against the hand you are using to clench, white-knuckled, the arm of his chair. Just like Tommy, the haircutter, pushes his privates against your arm while he cuts your hair. Except the dentist never meant for the little electric shock to run through my body every time his powder blue slacks brushed up against any part of my bare skin.

And yet I had to just sit there and not take him in my arms and throw his drill aside and cut into his being with my own, my very own drill. Maybe it's not Randy's size, but it'll do, I promise you.

And then, all too soon, the drilling stopped and Lawrence Lawrence Lawrence stepped back again fully into my view and smiled down at me with his clean white and perfect little teeth. And he held the mirror up for me to see that his work was as clean and white and perfect as he.

And then, imagine it, he told me that I should make an appointment with his nurse to come back next week and that I shouldn't bite down hard on anything until then. I promised I wouldn't, knowing that, given the right opportunity, big boy, it was a lie.

So we have a date next week. And one the week after for a thorough check-up and a cleaning, Lawrence Papsun, D.D.S., and I. And we will have appointments every week to doomsday if I have to open sodas with my teeth and leap out of windows jaw-first. And we will sit in restaurants sipping milk and get to know each other and then my arms will go akimbo.

And, bingo, he'll be mine.

I want to call Pixie and tell her my news. But it is not a good time. I want to call Benny, but I don't know where he is. So, instead, I pull the covers up to my neck, resettle the ice pack against my head and settle back in front of the TV. Bad Pee Wee is better than none.

30

I *am weightless. I am free. I am dizzy in space. I don't
know what I expected, really, from my first shuttle into
space. I guess I was always afraid that it would be like those
SciFi movies in the fifties, when the astronauts' mouths
were pulled down to their Adam's apples by the force of
four or five Gs.*

*But what I found was more like the revving of a giant
car. Like a child's toy that gets revved and revved higher
before the cord is pulled and the toy flies free.*

Off we went into space. Whoosh! Pop!

*And I am weightless. I am free. And I am dizzy with
delight in the midst of outer space.*

*As a free lance journalist and restaurant critic, I felt
that I didn't really have a chance when I entered the contest that would select the first journalist in space. But win
I did, with an entry entitled, "So You Want to Be an
Astronaut." And proud I am of this opportunity for new
experience.*

*I glance over at the captain of the mission, Captain
Papsun, who stares straight into the heart of the darkness
of space. He sits, gleaming in his silver space suit that shows
each rippling of his arm muscles as he lifts a hand to pull
a lever, push a button.*

*Our copilot, Sergeant Kasaba, has been ill-tempered
throughout our entire mission. Complaining first about
the ventilation system in the capsule and now about the*

food, as he pushes freeze-dried ice cream from the foil wrapper into his hungry gullet.

Captain Papsun, cool and remote, ignores the sergeant. Sticks strictly with the work at hand.

I, on the other hand, have unbuckled my seat belt and am floating free in outer space. Like Peter Pan. Here I am, an adult man who can fly, who will never grow up.

Over time, our quarters begin to feel a little cramped. Emotions tend to be worn a bit more on the sleeve. And Captain Papsun slowly begins to tell me about his life. About his childhood in the Swedish ghetto of Minnesota and his fierce determination to reach up to a better life. And with each bit of new knowledge, my respect for him grows.

For Sergeant Kasaba, however, I have nothing but contempt. For his spoiled veneer, for his hateful sneer. He wears the front of his space suit unzipped open nearly to the navel, showing a field of wild hair on his chest, through which he runs his huge hamlike hands. And he shows a neck covered in gold, with chains and pendants enough to offend even the cheapest Catskill comic.

Kasaba stands with his legs wide open, challenging. He never misses the opportunity to threaten Captain Papsun's fair and just rule of the ship.

This morning, the captain asked Kasaba to file computer reports requested by NASA. My reports, the findings of the first journalist in space.

Kasaba refused to do so. "I didn't come up in space just to be no secretary," he shouted, rubbing his hand across his nipples. The captain stepped forward to repeat the order. Kasaba again refused. Not wanting to be the cause of trouble, I stepped between the two men, although each dwarfed my lithe 5'10" body.

"Let me file the report, Captain," I said and started to move toward the keyboard.

"Get away from my fucking computer," Kasaba

*roared, shoving me hard. I fell upward, weightless, slam-
ming my head with great force against the wall of the
capsule. I put my hand to the injury, and came away
with a bloodied tooth that had been knocked forth by
the blow.*

*The blow, the blood, and the weightless condition
conspired against me, and I felt myself drifting away, hearing Captain Papsun, as if from a great distance, cursing
Kasaba and saying, "It's time for your space walk,
Sergeant."*

*With that, I heard the atmosphere rush into and out
of the airlock. And heard the clanking of Kasaba's magnetic
boots against the hull of the ship.*

*All was quiet for a brief moment. Beautifully quiet,
as I became aware of floating, floating in space. In one
brief instant, fear washed into me as I realized that this
was the only small pocket of light and heat and air in the
heavy dark canopy of space. That here we were in a very
fragile pocket of life in a most hostile environment. I must
have cried out in my delirium, for a moment later, I felt
a hand softly touch my cheek.*

*Captain Papsun had drawn close to me, let himself
float up to reach me. And, together, we were weightless. We
floated as he first touched my face and then as he tenderly
kissed my mouth, my mouth that pushed toward his, despite
the pain. We floated and bobbed in the air as he bared my
smooth, lightly muscled chest, and as I exposed his taut
abdominal ridge. And as our weighted boots crashed to
the floor.*

*This let us move higher and higher as our hands
enacted what our hearts had longed for all throughout this
long space flight.*

*And we remained weightless, intertwined, as we heard
Kasaba's knocking, at first as if from a great distance, and
then a pounding, pounding on the craft's hatch.*

And Captain Papsun kissed me again, with passion, with joy, with unspeakable longing as his hot manhood thrust toward me in the coldness of space.

"Pay him no attention," he said, "and maybe he'll just go away. . . ."

31

So there I was dividing my time between the two most important things: Arlene's Sweat It Out and my weekly appointments to have my teeth cleaned, bleached, buffed, filled, and anything else that needed to be done to them. I was in the dentist's chair more in the next few weeks that followed than I had been for the rest of my life put together.

And since I had decided that I was indeed the Hound of Hell, things got easier in terms of milking Randy for all the information I needed from him in order to steal Lawrence Papsun, D.D.S., right out from under his nose.

And he proved to be remarkably easy to pry open. In fact, it was at a candlelit interlude in a remote theatrical bar that, when I put my hand over his, he admitted to me, red-faced, that he was indeed attracted to me, as well as to other men.

I feigned surprise. But looked him straight in the eye and moved a little closer as if astounded by his admission and yet happy in my surprise.

As I knew he would, he pulled away and admitted to me also that he was involved with someone.

How I wanted to ask him if it were anyone I knew. But

I didn't. I looked him straight in the eye and mustered the appearance of great disappointment.

Then I told him that I was happy that we could just be friends.

In the days that followed, I would ask him little questions about his friend. What he did for a living. He was a professional person, Randy told me. What he liked and disliked in colors and food. He liked blue and gray and meat and potatoes and disliked orange and red and nouvelle cuisine. Whether he and his special friend lived together or not. They did not. And whether or not he saw this relationship as being potentially lifelong.

I asked Randy this one sunny winter day as we walked back to the church that housed Arlene's Sweat It Out, and where our cars were parked. We had gone uptown on foot to cool down after our exercise class. We had had a light lunch.

He asked me why I had asked such a question. He looked me straight in the eye with his own pale blue eyes. His vision was straight and direct.

I paused for a moment and then said, not altogether without honesty, that sometimes I wished he would just break up with the other guy and give me a chance. For some reason, when I was with Randy I could feel these things about him. Maybe it's just part of being a Hound of Hell, always being in heat.

He seemed so moved by the notion, that I was almost sorry to be manipulating him in such a way.

"I don't know sometimes if I even have a relationship that will last until the weekend. Sometimes it's just great and happy and I'm totally sure it is what I want and that it will last forever. Then other times, like this moment, I would just like to be free to do what I want to do, you know?"

I did know. And I did have to stop and consider the

possibilities. Of being involved with both Randy and Lawrence. Of repeating Pixie and Rollo. Not a good idea.

But he stood in front of me, with wintry steaming breath, looking so earnest and healthy and solid and real, that, in that moment, it was all I could do to keep from throwing my arms around him, although whether to kiss him or beg his forgiveness for what I intended to do I still am not sure.

Instead, after a moment, we shook hands to say our good-bye. "Look," said Randy, as we dropped hands, "I'm glad we met. If ever it didn't work out for me and Chip, well, I hope that I could call you . . . ."

I nodded that yes, of course, he should call. And it wasn't until a moment later that the name registered. Chip.

Who the hell was Chip?

32

I was still pondering the answer to that question the next morning when Mantis suddenly appeared by my side.

"Fauna would like to know why you have not been to see her," she said to me in her cloying singsongy voice.

Now, I did not want to answer her. Because I didn't see it as being any of her business why I hadn't kept my last two appointments with Fauna, most especially since the reason was rooted in money — I was, after all, running up some sort of dentist bill, way beyond anything my health insurance would cover. And also, I was growing tired of the way in which Fauna just sort of told me what I should be doing and not doing. I kind of missed the days when I did not know my future.

In fact, in my heart I had hung up my crystal. I didn't want anything more to do with Fauna, or with her confederate, Mantis. I had even secretly gone so far as to talk with my superior, Ms. Velchur, to try and get Mantis fired. But before I could bring the subject up, Ms. Velchur told me how very pleased she was with Mantis's work, and how she felt that I had hired a winner. So, no fool I, I held my tongue and went back to my office, where I sort of played a solo game of soccer with the hand of a mannequin.

And then Mantis appeared by my side to ask her question.

I didn't want to tell her the truth. I didn't want to tell her anything, in fact. So I just said that I would call Fauna and talk with her myself.

Maybe this pleased her, for she smiled at me slightly, as she'd taken to doing recently. But it was a smile without sweetness, one that didn't wrinkle her eyes. And she was gone as suddenly as she'd arrived.

I spent the rest of the day looking over my checkbook. In the past few days, I'd run up enough dental bills to cover two months' rent, and, with the appointments I'd already scheduled, I would be spending enough to buy myself the car that I desperately needed.

I would have to find a cheaper way to be near Lawrence.

Speaking of whom, who the hell was Chip?

If Randy was involved with a man named Chip, then why the hell was he kissing Lawrence Papsun, D.D.S., in the parking garage? And, if Randy were indeed involved with a man named Chip, did this mean that Lawrence was available? Or could I have possibly been standing behind the wrong car that fateful evening in the parking garage, in which case I had wasted the last six months for no good reason. In which case, I wondered what Orly Kasaba was doing for dinner.

Speaking of whom, I had not spoken to or heard from Orly or Pixie since the last time we'd all had dinner. Which left me guessing. Was I supposed to call and apologize for what I'd said? And how could I apologize? It would have been too much of a non sequitur. I couldn't just say that suddenly I had the compulsion to tell her that I'd slept with her brother and that it had all been a joke. And I couldn't tell her the truth, in that it would be adding insult to injury by hurting her in the present tense and not just in the pluperfect. And then there was the added threat of just what Orly would do to me if he ever found out — I mean, if he punched me that hard for just sleeping with Rollo, what would be his reaction to invading his own drunken coma?

Or maybe they were both just heartbroken about the whole thing. Sitting on the sofa just waiting for me to give them a call. Not knowing how to say they were sorry.

And the truth was, I was sorry, so very very sorry that the whole thing had happened, even the blow job by this time, truth to be told. For there's something sad about a blow job that can't be a conspiratorial tie between two guys. When it's a memory for one and a fear for the other. At least with Rollo I had a stupid but willing accomplice. With Orly, all I'd had was a hot corpse.

So I took stock of the situation as Dina had taught me to take stock of a situation. But I could not own up to the situation as Dina had taught me to own up to any situation. The cost was just too great. Although maybe the cost of silence was greater still.

At that moment, I picked up the phone and again dialed Dina's number. I had the number to her inner office, not the one that the nurse answered. I figured that again I could get her answering machine and hear the sound of her voice. That maybe just her message, her ''Hello, this is

Doctor Dutchman," said slowly and clearly and calmly, would give me a hint, an idea of how to continue.

But, after the third ring the telephone was answered by Dina herself. "Hello," she said. And then again, "Hello."

There was no way I could answer her, although I very much wanted to. Very much wanted to beg her to take me back, even if only for the fact that I still had almost three thousand bucks' worth of free mental care due me this year on my medical plan.

She said hello once more and then just hung up. Even her method of hanging up on what might have been an obscene telephone call was slow and calm. And I pictured her sitting there behind her neat little desk, under her healthy fern in her warm warm womb of an office, and it seemed, at that moment, even a better place to me than was my mother's kitchen on a cold winter's day, when the yellow walls and the scent of dinner made me feel whole and happy to be alive.

My office, Mantisized as it was with its newfound order and array, was no such haven. I ducked out of the basement entrance to the store and hurried down the mall to a tobacco shop, where I bought some harsh British cigarettes. And then I just walked. Strolled around the lower level and then up and down, from the restaurants on top to the banks and newsstands on the bottom.

Somewhere in the middle, as I was thinking of this as being a particularly uninspired and messy Wednesday, I saw Lawrence walking, reading his newspaper, oblivious as the day I'd first decided to love him.

I called to him and waved him over with the hand that held the lit cigarette.

When he came over, after his usual lag time of returning to the left-brained activity of speaking, he said, "You shouldn't smoke those. They stain the teeth."

I put it out. Telling him that he was right, of course.

And we walked a bit. And he told me that he didn't have any more patients that afternoon and that he was just hanging around the mall waiting to meet a friend.

I wanted to ask, "Who? Who? Who?" but restrained myself. Instead, I asked him if he wanted to get some cookies from the bakery one flight up.

His look told me that he didn't think we should be eating sugar, no matter how bad a day it was.

And I can't express how that look encompassed me. As if, by taking care of my teeth, he could take care of all the ills and troubles of my life, all my confusion and distortion.

And finally, we stopped walking and leaned over the center railing to look down at the ice skaters below on the lowest level, and I said to him, "You know, you remind me of an old friend from college. He looked so much like you. His name was Chip — Chip Govan."

And Lawrence just got the largest and whitest and cleanest smile on his face. "That's funny," he said, "because that's what all my friends call me. Chip."

Bingo, I thought. At least we got something cleared up today. And I looked him right in his blue-gray eyes, seeing the wrinkles around their edges that his true and warm smile had created.

"Then I hope you'll let me call you Chip," I said, returning his smile with one of my own and hoping my eyes were wrinkling.

33

Let's face it, in my dog-eat-dog line of work, you're only as good as your last display. Forget what I did for Christmas. Forget Back to School and all the rest. What Ms. Velchur remembered was that Mantis had worked magic with the sheets sheets sheets. And she wasn't about to let me forget it. Or the fact that I'd missed a couple of days in the past few weeks.

She seemed a bit placated when I told her of all the major dental work I'd had to have done and showed her my new fillings. But she also pointed out that Valentine's Day was here and she had high hopes for my work.

I asked her if I'd ever let her down and she didn't answer.

Let me tell you about Ms. Velchur. First, she looks just like her name sounds. Valerie Velchur. Navy blue business suits with the store's red carnation in her lapel. The flower, plastic, of course, is a store code. The middle management all wear red carnations. The big guys wear white.

So no matter what else she may be wearing, Ms. Velchur always has a red carnation over her left breast. Even in her nightgown, I'd imagine.

And the Ms. is her own appellation. She remains the only woman in this decade to still refer to herself in such a way, but so be it. She also has a Long Island accent and the longest fingernails I've ever seen. I suspect that they are the packaged kind, the kind that are given away as lovely parting gifts on all the television game shows.

But what sets Ms. Velchur apart from all the other middle managers are her shoes. For she wears the highest, thinnest stiletto pumps that have ever been seen outside the warehouse district of New York City. These are not just Fuck Me shoes, they are Fuck Me Right Here and Now shoes. The sort of shoes that the ancient Orientals would have devised. They force her to walk in a slow sinewy tumble of a step. They have every other man in the store interested and they refer to her as "The Feet." As in here come The Feet. And then everyone who has not been working at all for the last half hour quickly rushes off to get to work, because they all know that she can't move fast enough in those shoes to catch them not working. And they all know how great those shoes make her legs look under her sensible and businesslike suit.

Everyone in the store wants to know what Ms. Velchur does after work. But she has chosen a name that does not even give us a hint as to whether or not she does what she does after work alone or with a steady companion.

Now, the other thing that these shoes do for Ms. Velchur is make her taller than I am. Something that upsets me no end, as I rather prefer that all women and most men look straight into my Adam's apple or collar bone when they try to talk to me. Only the men I want to sleep with should be taller than I, and then only slightly. But I must look up when I talk to Ms. Velchur, or rather when I nod in agreement as she talks.

And I agree to do a bang-up Valentine's Day display.

I have decided to call up Pixie and sing, "Angst for the Memories," and make her love me again just a little. But not today. Tomorrow.

Tomorrow.

I got a postcard from Benny from a place he refers to as Pirhanna del Rio. He says that he and the King are having the time of their life, but that Thallassa is in major depression and shock having mooned over a machismo Hispanic sailor during their tour of the South Seas. Seems he knew more uses for leather than she but was caught in the act of showing them to another sailor instead. Thallassa, he says, is wearing white in mourning for her heart. He also says that there is gold in them there hills and he means to get it.

Perhaps this means that they are moving west with the act. Who knows?

No return address.

Mantis, in the short meantime of my meeting with Ms. Velchur and my stopping to read my mail, has designed a concept for Valentine's Day sales. She is turning the women's clothing department into a giant Valentine's Day box, like we used to make in elementary school. Huge Valentines are in perpetual motion toward being dropped in the box. "Be Mine," they beg. What they mean is, be a good shopper. She also wants to have a "best valentine" contest.

I am just making a face over the idea when Ms. Velchur sticks her red-carnationed upper body through our doorway and says she heard the idea from outside the door. Brilliant and innovative are the words she uses, instead of the sucko and derivative that I had planned to use.

And so Mantis takes over the Valentine's display.

Discouraged, I go for another in a long line of long walks through the mall. I buy my British cigarettes again and then stop to look at the cards that the newsstand has up front. I find a valentine covered with red and gold and dainty white lace and buy it. Outside the store, I stop to sign the card,

"A friend," and then add a caret between the words and write in the word "special" between the other two.

I then seal the envelope and write "Chip Papsun, D.D.S." on the red envelope, along with the address that I've already memorized. I am careful to write all this with my left hand so that he will not connect this penmanship with what he finds signing the checks that pay his bills.

I fish a stamp out of my wallet, where I keep stamps instead of Trojans, I am sad to admit. And I drop the envelope into the mailbox by the front of the mall.

I do this to send a secret message of affection. I do it to somehow, in some small way, feel connected.

34

When Ms. Velchur calls me into her office at the beginning of February, a particularly bad February, one that is filled with snow and sleet and grayness, I know that it is for no reason that I will enjoy. I know that we are not going to talk about Easter displays.

Even before I walk into her office, even before I sit down facing her, with her head raised above mine, the traveling pain begins in my left elbow and moves down the arm and across my chest and abdomen.

How am I going to support my Mr. Goodtooth habit?

Ms. Velchur leans across her desk toward me. Her look is severe. "I think it's time we had a little talk, Wyatt."

I just look at her, my vision blurring slightly.

"You've been with our company for what — three years now?"

"Yes. Three years. Yes," I answer thinking of all the holidays that were contained within those three years, all the fishing line and tinsel that those months contained.

"And while I am aware that you were hired not by me but by my predecessor, Mr. Willis, I do think that we've always had a good rapport, don't you?"

"Yes, I certainly would say so. Yes, yes, we do."

"Then I just want to be very honest with you. I can't help but have noticed that your work has been slipping of late. And that if it weren't for the very fine help you've been given in your department by your new assistant, our store would have had some very weak displays in recent months.

"Display is an integral part of our overall marketing concept. We cannot afford to let our efforts slide in the day of television — of bright lights and quick colors. It is all the more important these days that we compete effectively for the shoppers' dollars.

"But I'll get to the point. . . ."

Here she paused a moment to walk around and sit on the front of the desk. In that moment, as Fauna would say, my aural self rose above my body. It was as if I were sitting on the ceiling looking down on someone playing me in a bad theatrical production. From this vantage point, I could not only see and hear as before, but could also notice, for the first time, just how thin Ms. Velchur's hair was getting on top.

"I'm putting you on warning and giving you just one more chance to pull your department together. To put an end to your mysterious disappearances and to show me that you have begun once again to care about the quality of your work.

"While I have in the past thrilled to your work, I want to let you know that it is going to be necessary for me to absolutely thrill to it once again, and quickly, for me not to have to take some sort of drastic action."

She walked again around to the back of her desk.

"Is all this very clear?" she asked me.

My aural self popped back in just in time for us both to slowly nod. "Yes, Yes, it is. Yes."

"All right then," she concluded, "I sincerely hope that next time we speak it will be for happier reasons."

I rose and half backed out the door. Once outside, the smile I'd kept frozen on my face faded somewhat — like a rose in the snow. I knew that I couldn't possibly afford at this time to lose this job, what with all the dental bills and all. And I knew that I couldn't go back to my office right now, because I would open my mouth and ask Mantis for advice, which was just the sort of an in that the little Eve Harrington bitch was looking for. And I couldn't go to Fauna for advice, since that was as bad if not worse than telling Mantis. And I couldn't talk to Benny because I didn't even know where he was. And I couldn't talk to Orly or Pixie without risking physical harm.

Which left me pretty much bereft. Until I remembered the business card on which Randy'd written Chip's number, and I dug it out and turned it back over and there was Randy's office number.

When I called him, I must have sounded sufficiently upset, because he agreed to meet me at the bar on the mall's second level.

As it was after two P.M., happy hour had already begun. So I filled one of those little white paper plates with the cocktail wieners in puff pastry and sat down at a booth and ordered a drink. Gin, of course. I had eaten about five of the wieners and had traced the initials that had been carved into the slab top of the booth when Randy arrived.

The fact that I waved him over so blatantly betrayed the fact that I had already had a bit to drink.

But he sat down and ordered up. I went over to the food bar to fill the plate again and also brought Randy a little white paper plate heaped with the very orange cheese that seems to frequent happy hours and museum openings.

Then I told him my story.

Well, not all of it, just how Mantis was doing her inscrutable best to undermine me at work and how I'd been called on the carpet for the first time in my life and how my job was hanging by a thread. I left out all the information about Chip, I always did leave out all the information about Chip, except for the day at Arlene's Sweat It Out when he asked about how I'd made out at the dentist, and I told him that I had decided, at the last minute, to go to my usual dentist.

So Randy leveled one of his faded blue stares at me and told me that I had to make up my mind not to give up this job to Mantis without a fight. Unless, of course, I had money in the bank, which, of course, I didn't. He reminded me that I had the upper hand in the situation, even if Ms. Velchur would not let me fire that bitch goddess Mantis, and even if it seemed suddenly that every woman on earth was ganging up on me.

"What can you do about it?" he asked me. "What kind of display could you put together to just blow them all out of the water?"

So we kicked around themes. Romulus and Remus, we decided, was all wrong for the audience we were trying to reach. Ditto Dido and Aneas, since it ended with her on a funeral pyre. Which also left out most other famous pairs of lovers, in that one of them always seems to end up dead. Even Romeo and Juliet, although we kicked this around long enough for me to pull my foot out of my shoe and begin to slowly draw a line with my big toe up the inside of his pant leg.

Randy neither pulled his leg away nor returned my probing pressure. We decided that Romeo and Juliet had been done to death, you should excuse the pun, and we continued on to other lovers. Dante and Beatrice were too obscure. The Duke and Duchess of Windsor were too wimpy and physically unattractive.

Somewhere in there, along about the fourth or fifth drink, the idea of Rudolph Valentino came up. I think it was my idea, but I cannot be sure it was. But we both agreed that this was the perfect idea. Valentino, whose name even sounded like Valentine. Whose image evokes wild passion and high drama. And who was the closet case of all time. This particularly appealed to both Randy and me — especially to Randy, who by now had spread his legs beneath the table and was letting me occasionally run my foot up his crotch. He would let me rest it there and squeeze his genitals for just the briefest of moments, however, before he issued a high-pitched giggle that sent his organ withering and my foot back to the floor.

After about a half hour of terrific Valentino ideas — I drew the concepts on the empty paper plates that were filling the table — Randy leaned close to me as I put the finishing touches on a tango motif.

"I want you to know," he said with a slight slur, "that if you ever need money I'd be very pleased to give it to you."

Now this was some sort of turning point for me. Not that I decided not to go after the man's boyfriend, but some defense of mine, some wall around my heart, was pierced by this simple sentence. I looked back at Randy's bland young face and almost started to cry. At the pleasure of knowing that someone would not sit idly by while I sank beneath the waves that were threatening to drown me. And at the sorrow of knowing that, like me, Randy was pretty damned sure that I had waited a little too late to decide to worry about my career.

But still, we had an abundance of paper plates. A wonderful world of Rudolph Valentino. And if Valentino didn't work, well, maybe just as many sobbing women would come to my funeral as went to his.

After Randy made his kind sweet dear little offer, I slipped my foot back into my shoe and watched as he paid the tab. Then we walked out of the restaurant together, keeping each other going through sheer willpower and hope.

I walked with him to his car, parked up many levels on the roof of the mall in the parking garage. I was not at all surprised to see that he drove a Saab. I stood close by and watched him get in the driver's side. And stood longer by the passenger window, just looking in. Slowly, very slowly, or so it seemed, Randy reached over and flipped the lock on the passenger door. And even more slowly, I opened the door and climbed inside.

I ran my fingertips along the leather of the seats as I lowered my body weight into the car, and then lifted my fingers to just barely brush Randy's jawline, his cheek, his lips.

Then I moved my face closer and closer to his. It was not as if we were pulled together by some spark of energy, by some chemical reaction, but it was as if the seemingly passive force of gravity was slowly pulling our bodies down to one another.

When our lips met, it was with a soft and tender warmth. And slowly our lips parted and I felt the slickness of his tongue slowly invade my mouth. Felt that tongue slide across the front of my lower teeth, teeth that had been made clean and slick and white by the hands of Randy's lover.

Sheer gravity slowly moved my head in a circular pattern, moving, sliding to my right. Randy's face slid softly left. Our lips parted and we leaned, like two dolls at rest, him with his head on the leather back of his chair, me with my head resting between his jaw and his shoulder.

There was a long pause, broken only by the sound of a car door opening, somewhere, somewhere far away. "Thank you," I said to Randy, kissing him on his ear, meaning to thank him for the drinks, the kiss and his belief in me. And then I slowly unwound my body from his, slowly pulled away.

And I opened the car door and got out and walked away. I entered the mall again and never heard him start his engine.

The time was about seven P.M. My pockets were filled with paper plates. All these new ideas, as original and staggering as any I'd ever had before. This was my ticket, I was sure, back to the top of the display heap.

I walked back into my store, intending to go right to my office when I saw all the huge valentines hanging about the store on fishing line.

Mantis had beaten me to the punch again through sheer speed. "Be Mine" was everywhere. Not a new concept, but certainly a large one.

I went back to my office to get my coat. This time I was beaten, there was no doubt about it. But I got no more than ten steps toward my office when I heard The Feet tapping up behind me.

"In my office," was all she said.

Well, what choice did I have but to follow her? I sat back down where I'd sat only hours earlier and tried to look her in the eye, but couldn't.

"I tried to find you hours ago and your assistant told me that you'd left. Again. After I'd warned you once. And now I see you returning at seven o'clock, after your assistant worked for hours to finish the Valentine's Day display, which I had told you was your last chance. I told you I wanted you to get out there and win me over again with this display and then, when I come to see what you've accomplished, I find your assistant doing your work for you again. What do you have to say for yourself?"

I got the paper plates, a little worse for the folding, out of my coat pocket to show her my Valentino ideas. I hadn't noticed, in the somewhat darkened bar, just how catsup-smeared they were. In this bright fluorescent light, they looked more like doodles than schematics.

There was a moment's shock on her face. "You've been out drinking," she said. I couldn't tell if it was a question or a flat-out declaration.

I looked up at her towering figure, trying to find her eyes, but the ceiling light was too bright, casting her in silhouette as she marched her form about the room.

"If you're going to give your assistant your work to do, she might as well get your salary, too. Go clear out your things. We'll give you two weeks' severance, but just get out tonight."

I put my hand to my mouth, trying not to cry. My knees would not solidify enough to lift me from the chair.

Again she looked down at me. "Do you want me to call security?"

My knees snapped to at the notion of such humiliation. I rose smoothly and wished that I'd drunk enough to vomit on her rug.

"I guess there's nothing to say," I managed.

"Except good-bye," was all she answered.

I don't even remember the ride home, and yet I made it without hitting a tree. Try though I would.

I kept expecting that everything would look different after such a disaster had struck. That the town would look hurricane-ravaged, tornado-struck. That my car would be buried under rubble, that my apartment would have been robbed.

And so it was something of a shock and a puzzle for me to find everything so much the way it had always been before. So normal. To unlock my apartment door and find the same white walls and movie posters. The same little plaid couch that pulled out to make the living room a spare bedroom.

I haven't described my apartment. But that has not been through oversight, but out of a sense of embarrassment. I was raised with the notion that money can't buy taste, and that is certainly true. But also true is the reality that taste is worthless without money. For this apartment, a somewhat seedy one-bedroom in an old building whose elevator never works, has been pulled together at garage sales and flea markets. Everything works or nearly does. The aging color TV with its garish sixties color and rabbit ears. The toaster that toasts only one side of the bread at a time.

I've always been hesitant to let anyone see my apartment. Mostly because, given my outlandish displays — the displays that I USED to get to make, most people would expect my apartment to be something special. But it's not — it is the domicile of millions of widows on Social Security.

I looked over at the answering machine that I got for Christmas from my mother who was sick of never being able to reach me. The little red light was flashing that I had a message.

I walked over and pushed "Playback." The tape whirled.

"This is Fauna," the voice said, as if she had to identify herself. As if I didn't know her voice by now. "I won't even bother to suggest that you call me back. I know that that's a waste of effort. So, I just wanted you to be aware that your planets are all square with one another. Just don't do anything, OK? This is a real critical time for you, so just lay low."

I turned the switch back to "Answer" and sat down on

the couch facing the machine, listening to it click back into answer mode. And I just began to shake my head slowly, still reeling from the shock and the kiss and the gin.

Now she would have to be right about something, after having talked ozone for weeks. Now she would have to hit the nail on the head.

35

Stardate 2727/56
Dear Dream Diary,

I am Norm again, but this time I am dressed in a tuxedo with my toolbelt pulled up high and tight like a cummerbund.

I am holding a champagne glass in my hand, but it is filled with sawdust instead of alcohol. I am standing in the empty living room of a house at the Cape. I can hear the ocean through the open windows.

It is a warm summer evening. I hear the call of seagulls and smell the scent of salt in the air. There is a gentle lulling, a pull of quiet harmony as some quiet strain of music blows into the room through that open window.

This house is done. Restored and completed. There is the vague feeling in this dream that this is the last house I will ever have to work on. That, after having worked for so many others, I have finally finished my own home. The floor planks are wide and smooth beneath my feet. There is a stone fireplace and one broad chandelier that tinkles and turns in the gentle breeze.

I turn around and the music that I have heard is inside the room. A band plays in the corner, gentle jazz rhythms. And I hear myself sigh.

Suddenly, the room is filled. With Pixie, who is dressed all in pink. And Orly in his New Year's tuxedo. And Thallassa, who wears a soft shimmering gown, covered with a shawl against the ocean chill. And Benny, who has lost weight and who is dressed in every color but black. And Lawrence Papsun, D.D.S., who pats me softly on the back. And Randy, who pulls up close to me and whispers that he understands before he takes Chip's hand from his own and places it in mine. And Mantis, who walks in last through the front door in a green chiffon gown and wraps her neck around my neck and asks me to forgive.

I toss the sawdust within my glass into the air, but it does not fall back to the ground. It swirls in the air, becomes a mist.

Dina and Fauna come down the stairs from above. They are talking and standing close close together. I notice suddenly that they are Siamese twins. Joined first at the hip and then at the hand. They're dancing together to the smooth jazzy music.

I am turning my neck, rolling my head, feeling my capillaries relax with the motion, the slow slow undulating motion. And everyone is dancing. All together with each other.

And, like in *Carrie,* the house starts rumbling, the walls start rolling inward, like my head across my neck. And as my arms rise up slowly, the foundations squeal with delight and the support beams dip from heaven.

My house is me, a black hole. A collapsing, screaming mess that can't forgive Mantis or anyone, anyone, that is held together with chicken wire, almost invisible, and with thin nylon fishing line.

The walls, as they collapse, as they crush me — for

everyone else has managed to walk very slowly to freedom, although my mad dashing, my expenditure of all my mortal energy won't get me across the room — the walls bear the legend in bright red: "Be Mine."

And the sawdust raises up a torrent and rains back down on the earth below.

36

Of course, the day after you get fired, the hardest thing to do is just simply to get out of bed. Which is why I didn't bother, I just stayed there, my legs wrapped in the sheets trying to figure out what gives.

And I'm lying there trying to figure out what went wrong. I mean, I'm thirty-something, for God's sake, one of the trendy folk, one of the cool. Knowing all the while that I'm about as cool as a suppository.

By this time, I've been awake at least twenty minutes, and yet it's four hours until *Days of Our Lives*. What to do?

So I pondered the situation for about an hour. How I had now kissed the man whose lover I intend to steal. How now I am not sure just which of the two I want to steal from the other. How I don't know how the hell I'm supposed to pay the fleet of dental bills that I will be receiving in the next two weeks. Or how I'm supposed to steal away a man I owe hundreds and hundreds of dollars to. Or how I'm supposed to pay for anything else besides these bills, either. Or how I'm going to survive, what with maybe $157 in the bank, if my addition is right, which it almost never is. Or how I'm going to survive after the next two weeks are up, for which I am receiving severance pay, which is, in my opinion, another word for charity. Which is also OK. Everything is that puts money in your pockets.

And I thought how everything would seem better if Benny were here, as he would have an immediate scheme of some vile sort or other. Or if Dina were within scream-ing range, because she would make it seem to be a challenge — that's how she would refer to it. "Wildroot," she'd say, "you are facing a special challenge." And I could get caught up in the challenge of it all, in the swash-buckling, and I wouldn't have to deal with the fact that I'm going to be left selling matchsticks on New Year's Eve. And that they're going to find my tattered and frozen little body in the doorway to the mall, lifeless, on New Year's Day.

Could I get unemployment after having been fired, I wanted to know. How did I get welfare?

After all, I'd tricked one store in this whole metropolitan area into giving me a job, and, for a long while, they'd actually bought my act, applauded my efforts, but now, after Ms. Velchur slurred my name throughout the small puddle that was retail, what hope did I have of fooling anyone else?

Before you know it, I realized, I would find myself behind the counter working in fast-food servicing, which was not only the lowest-paying and least-rewarding form of work available in the whole country, but its employees were the least humane. I could just imagine myself cheerily taking the fries from the deep fat and dumping them into one of those thermal lighted bins and then tossing the salt all over their golden brown bodies. I pictured my complexion after one week of working near deep fat. I was unnerved.

And, after I had run through the litany of fears, com-plete with the side order of self-hatred for having taken an art degree rather than having studied to be something useful like a janitor, I decided to seek after the wise counsel that could unleash upon me the second great engine that drove my life — along with fear — guilt.

The guilt began when I had to get out my phone directory to look up the telephone number.

I dialed. The fact that it was long distance fed the fear machine. And midday and midweek, for the highest possible expense. This was going to be good.

The phone on the other end rang, thousands of miles away. Once. Twice. Three times. "Oh no. Oh God. Oh no," I prayed, not wishing to have to whip my spirits up to this frenzy later to again start the twin engines revving.

At the seventh ring, I decided to give it just one more. Had I used the operator, she would have said by now, "There's no one home, try later." And I would have answered, "It always takes a while here, just keep on ringing." The operator would have sighed.

Eight rings. Nine. I might as well face it, no one is home. And then the miracle: "Hello?"

Always with the question mark. Always with the trembling voice. Telephone calls, particularly those with the hollow long distance sound at the other end, could only bring bad news.

"Hello, Mother," I said evenly, wanting to get her as calm as possible.

"Wyatt?" she shouted. She always shouted at long distance.

"Yes Mother, it's me."

"What's wrong, Wyatt?"

"Nothing. I just wanted to hear your voice."

"What's wrong?"

"Nothing, really. I'm just a little homesick for you."

"What's wrong?"

"I got fired."

There, I'd said it and I was glad. After all, I HAD called

her to give her this news. To find out what she would have
to say about it.

"When?" she asked in a thunderstricken whisper.

"Yesterday. It just happened yesterday."

"So you don't know what you're going to do yet?"

"No, it just happened yesterday."

"Come home."

"That's sweet, Ma, but I can't come home right now."

"You just come right on home."

Now, when my father had died, home ceased to be the
large white house that I'd grown up in and had, instead,
become a small one-bedroom condo about two or three
miles away from my mother's sister, Aunt Bessie. I had no
intention of going home, where, in stereo yet, I could hear
how disappointed my whole family was with me.

By now the telephone call had gone on about ten
minutes. My financial fears were growing.

"How did it happen?" she asked me.

"I don't know. I have a new boss. A woman. I don't
think she ever liked me."

"Well then, why don't you just come home?"

"Ma, you don't have any room for me even if I wanted
to come home. I'm thirty-one years old. I can't just go home
every time I lose my job."

"We'll put a cot in the living room."

"Look, I've got to work this out for myself. I'll just find
a new job and get started again. Maybe I'll try something
else."

"We have jobs here. You just get on a bus and come right
home."

"Mother. . . ."

"I'm only trying to help you. Do you want me to come
there?"

"No, really, I'm all right."

"You want me to call that boss of yours?"

"No, I think that it's really too late for anything to happen at the store."

"I have some money in the bank. I'm going to send you some money."

"No, that's really not necessary. I've got money. Besides, I should be sending you money. You don't have any money."

"I've got enough. Are you eating?"

"I'm eating fine. I've only been out of work for twelve hours. And I get two more weeks' pay. Then I'll get unemployment."

"Not if you got fired. You don't get unemployment if you get fired."

"Don't worry, I'll work it out. I'm an adult and adults can work things out."

"My God, you'll be on welfare next. Come home right now. I'll send you the ticket for the bus."

"Mother, look, I'm not coming home and if you send me a ticket, I'll just send it right back to you."

"Then I'm sending you some food money."

"I'll tear up the check, Mother. I swear to you that I'll just tear it right up."

By now I'm feeling feverish. I can tell a guilt rush is building.

There's a quaver in her voice. "I can't just leave you there not eating. Let me help. Just because I'm old . . . ."

"You're not that old, Mother. I just really don't need —"

"— I always thought things would be so different before your father died. I thought that in my old age you'd come over to the house and bring your children and we'd all sit on the porch in the sun."

Here was the guilt rush beginning, sweeping.

"You remember how nice the sun was on the side porch, with the breeze blowing? I guess it's a blessing now that you never found the right girl and got married. What with your not being able to keep a job and all . . . ."

There was a pause during which we each went to our corners to be wiped down with a damp rag.

"Ma?" I finally said.

"Yes?"

"I'm sorry about calling you and getting you worried. Everything's fine. Really it is."

"I just wish you'd come on home. Just for a visit." I could hear soft tears collecting at the back of her throat.

"I will, Mother, in just a few weeks. Just as soon as I've sorted things out. Then we'll have a visit when I come to take you out dancing."

I could hear her try to laugh a bit at this.

"Look Mother," I continued, "I had better go now. This is costing me an arm and a leg."

"I'll send you the money for the phone call."

"No, really, that's not what I meant."

"No, really —"

"No, really, I just wanted to hear your voice."

"Are you sure that you have everything you need?"

"Yes, everything. I have to go, Mother."

"Wyatt?"

"Yes, Mother?"

"Why haven't you ever got married?"

"Because I haven't found anyone as nice as you, Mother. I love you."

"I love you, too, son. I'm sending you the money for this call."

And then she hung up.

Of course, by the time this conversation had ended, I was no longer in the mood for *Days of Our Lives*. The clock told me that I could just make it to Arlene's Sweat It Out if I hurried. But I found that I couldn't do that either. Randy would be there, and after the kiss in the parking lot,

I wouldn't know what to say to him, just like I didn't know what to say to Pixie, Orly, Benny, Fauna, or Dina.

I looked out the window to a snowy, sleety February day to realize that I wouldn't have to wait eleven months to freeze in the snow while selling matches.

In the hours that followed, I turned the television on and off, made and ate my lunch, and dusted the coffee table. I also made three telephone calls and then hung up before they were answered. Twice I decided to go over to the store to get my severance check. But there was plenty of time for that tomorrow.

I sat on my checked couch, the yellow and green plaid seeming ever more revolting, the couch itself ever more tattered. The walls were closing in. Ice white, just like the outdoors.

I ended up in the bathroom, reading *People* magazine.

I flipped through the picks and pans feeling like the biggest pan of all. Went on to this week's article on Princess Di.

Turning the page from her, I found myself face to face with a soap opera stud named Stanley Dumon, played by Sean, the actor I'd loved in my twenties. I always thought that we would meet again, but never, in my wildest dreams, did I think that it would happen with me in a bathroom and him in the pages of *People* magazine.

But there he was, posing with his shirt off and with a much better build than I had ever seen below his neck. The article called him a "beefcake bombshell," and the "Paul Newman of Daytime."

In the copy it said that he was dating an actress on the same show. Yeah. Sure. Right.

I felt like calling Marvin Mitchelson and suing for palimony. I mean, it worked for the guy who was supposed to have been Liberace's bodyguard, didn't it? And, I mean, we were talking big bucks potentially here, right? And fame — my own name in *People,* right where it belonged.

Then people would be calling me to get back into my life. Even Pixie. Hell, I might even hear from old Rollo.

And I deserved the money, right? After all, I'd stopped my own design career just to help him get launched in show business. That's what got me started in retail in the first place, getting him started in show business. And look where it had gotten me. Sitting in the bathroom reading about other people's lives — even make-believe lives like this one if they expected me to believe that he was dating a woman.

And I got pretty much worked up with this notion and even, for a brief moment, thought of the relationship I'd had with Sean — the only real relationship I'd ever had, really — as money in the bank. As an investment I'd made years ago to pay off for me right now.

But then I pictured my mother opening her weekly copy of the *National Star* and seeing an article on the palimony suit, complete with a picture of me in court pointing a finger at Sean. And I pictured her clutching her chest in pain. And I knew I'd never bother to do it, or even to ever get in touch with Sean again.

And I looked back at the picture of Sean, so muscular, smooth in this shirtless picture, so glossy and oiled. And then I thought of better times, of erotic moments.

And I slowly, carefully tore the picture out of the magazine without ripping it.

And then I jerked off into it and felt surprisingly better.

37

February 15

Dear Diary,

Well, Valentine's Day has come and gone and I received only one card. A Valentine from my mother with a check for $150 in it. I returned the check in a letter telling her that I am considering the Peace Corps, but that I would visit her before shipping out.

I hope that calms her somewhat.

Other than that no mail, except for a white envelope from Lawrence Papsun, D.D.S. When the envelope arrived, I hoped for one wild moment that it might be a personal note of some kind. Instead, it is the letter that I have been dreading — a bill for $1,200, and a reminder that I have another appointment this Friday. I may as well go and owe him another hundred or so. So what?

I do not believe for a moment that Marlena is really dead on *Days of Our Lives*. She will be back, just when Roman least expects it. At least after her nighttime series folds.

In lieu of Arlene's Sweat It Out, I have been putting Linda Ronstadt's "Mad Love" on my old stereo and waving my arms and lifting my knees in my own living room. From a TV show, I learned not to put my arms behind my head when doing sit-ups, but to cross them over my chest. I have also learned several new recipes, although I have eaten nothing except pizza that I can get delivered. In fact, I was amazed, upon looking in the phone book, at all the things you can get delivered to you. But I'm sticking with pizza. I am, in fact, on a first-name basis with the delivery boy, Justin, who, if he would do something to clear up his skin, would not be bad looking, only statutory rape. Because the boy is not eighteen yet.

February 16
Dear Diary,

In today's mail, I got my severance check. No note, no comment, nothing. Like I was a number on the computer and now that number's been wiped out.

Learned about new and innovative ways to make chili from a morning talk show, and heard a number of women speak up about marital rape on Geraldo Rivera's show. Geraldo's face, I could not help but notice, is wrinkling up like a prune.

Got sick of the marital rape and turned over to Sally Jesse Raphael, who had on a couple of gay men and a fat woman who all together were raising a family that they somehow produced among them from natural processes. Wished that I had turned the show on sooner to find out who had diddled whom.

This afternoon, both Oprah and Phil have Elizabeth Taylor, who is bound to talk about Rock Hudson, as well as her own weight loss, on at least one of these shows. Wish to hell I'd bought a VCR when I still had a store discount.

February 17
Dear Diary,

So I finally went outside today, since Justin told me yesterday that he thought there was a trace of springtime in the air. Springtime in the Yukon maybe. It was not more than twenty degrees outside. Which meant that I had to wait a good five minutes before my Datsun would turn over, in that it does not get this cold in Japan and the car makers have no concept of Eastern reality, as they are buying up California and Hawaii and not Maryland or New Jersey.

So, I went to the bank, where I cashed my check and took all the money out with me, leaving the $157 still in the bank. And with the cash, I went out and bought a whole bunch of cans of tuna and a copy of a magazine called *Buttfucker's Monthly* from one of these really seedy newsstands on the wrong side of town. As usual when I (rarely) buy one of these magazines — the kind that have the "anal act" right on the cover, but with a small black rectangle covering the zone of impact — I faked a coughing fit while they rang the thing up, having already hidden it between a copy of *People* (another copy of the issue with Sean in it, this one to keep as I no longer have that other photo) and a copy of *The Atlantic.* I have learned through years of practice never to put the filthy rag on the bottom, as the storekeeper will surely move it to the top of the pile as he rings the magazines up, and will then flash it to everyone in the shop while he is bagging your purchases. If you put it in the middle, however, greed to get your money will overcome his need to flash and he will just bag the damned things. The coughing fit allows you not to have to connect eyes with the guy who is working the counter. They usually have cigars and they always leer at anyone who buys *Buttfucker's.*

So I went home with my purchases. Going in the front door, I was struck by the notion that my apartment should be damned neat and tidy now that all I had to do was stay at home. Unfortunately, it seemed to be a greater excuse to ravage than it was to dust. The pizza boxes alone seemed to be stacking up to the kitchen ceiling. I ignored the mess and opened a can of tuna. I got a fork and went into the bedroom just in time to catch the end of Oprah, who was hosting yet another one of those shows about women who can't lose weight.

After that, I waved my arms around to "Mad Love."

February 18

Dear Diary,

So I went back to Arlene's Sweat It Out today after I noticed a new roll of fat forming around my middle as a result of all that pizza and all that Oprah.

Of course the first thing I noticed is that Randy looks a little pale to me. A little nervous to see me. And the bald man hasn't been back for weeks.

In the showers, I try to open lines of communication with Randy slowly by asking about the bald man. Randy tells me that he heard that the bald man ran off with a hairdresser.

Then he asks me about work. And I tell him the whole Wonderful World of Irony. He sits down on the bench next to me while we talk and puts his hand on my bare knee as a gesture of support. He again mentions his willingness to be of financial help.

This makes my brain all funny again — both the knee and the offer — and I lean over slightly toward him. Abruptly, Randy pulls away and stands above me. Thinking that he has other things besides kissing in mind, I lean forward toward him and pull away the towel that he has wrapped around his clean showered waist.

"No," is all he says. The simple flat syllable. A gesture of his right hand matches his verbal comment. There is no jumping back, no surprise, no lack of sureness. And then he continues, "I can't. I told you I was involved with someone else."

After that, we talked a bit about being friends and really how that was the best sort of relationship anyway. And I figured that I'd end up spending the evening with my

Buttfucker's instead of with Randy. And that seemed OK to me, really. And then he asked me out to dinner, out of the clear blue sky. I guess he felt sorry for me or something. Maybe it was because he turned his back to me when he dropped his towel to get dressed, suddenly shy. After having had no problem displaying his huge member to a stranger and then to a friend who he'd never kissed. How strange that one kiss in a parking garage could make so much difference.

And so he asked me to dinner. Of course, I said yes. Free food and a cute guy. I even sort of understood about his rejection of me, would have sort of been shocked if I weren't rejected by this time. Me being a Hound of Hell and all.

Over dinner (in the mall, of course, but at the very best restaurant), Randy was a little wistful. We drank wine and he told me about how things were going at his office until he realized that this might cause me pain, in that I didn't have an office of my own right now, and suddenly he got a look on his face like someone at a dinner party would if they'd just told a Polish joke and then found out your name was Romansky. But I told him it was OK and that I was really very interested in all that went on at his office, which is one of those investment houses that has a whole bunch of people's names, all starting with the letter "W."

Then, after dinner and after Randy had paid the tab, we went walking through the mall. And we ended up in front of my old store. "Let's go in," I said.

"I don't think you really want to," Randy responded. But I grabbed him by the crook of the arm and dragged him through the doorway. He acted, while walking with me, as if he were touring Israel with Hitler. Like at any moment armed guards would come and eject us from the store.

But me, I was lost in amazement at the new displays. There were dinosaurs everywhere around the place. "Dinosaur Days — the largest savings in history," said a large red and green banner. I was so amazed at the transformation that had been made in just these few days that I failed to notice the sound of "The Feet" approaching us from behind.

"Wyatt," said Ms. Velchur, "what are you doing back in this store?"

I turned around to face her. She had showdown written across her forehead. What she didn't take into account, however, is that, since firing me, she had already lost all authority over me. What fear I used to feel in facing her was replaced with a nice clean sense of freedom.

"I am back in this store as a shopper, Ms. Velchur, along with my friend." I gestured to Randy, who stood slightly behind me. "We have come to look at the VCRs that you've advertised as being on sale. If you will excuse us. . . ."

Nonplused, and I mean definitely nonplused, Ms. Velchur stepped to the side to let me pass. She would, I knew, never interfere with a potential purchase. Randy and I walked toward the down escalator. But, after a few steps, I turned around and spontaneously did something that I have always wanted to do. For the sheer malice and joy of it. I walked back to Ms. Velchur and pulled the red carnation from her gray suit and threw it on the floor. Then I mashed it with the toe of my right shoe. Then we went down the escalator.

38

When I was a little kid, there was this stuff, a toy really, called Lightning Bug Glow Juice. It came in a jar like the soap stuff that we used to make soap bubbles, but this was more like paint. It was that same green color as the paint that they used to make watch faces glow in the dark. And it was really the same stuff. You just painted it on whatever — I usually would paint it over the bones in my hand — and then you would hold the painted object, or bones or whatever under a light and it would absorb the light and then glow for a few minutes.

It was often used to make obscenities glow off the walls in our back alley.

Well, these things that I am writing about here, these are the moments in my life that have been painted with Lightning Bug Glow Juice. These are the moments, out of all the collected many many moments, that stand out, that glow when placed next to the usual dull experiences. . . .

PART THREE

"I've always been a private person.
I've never wanted to write a book...."
— Rock Hudson

39

When Randy and I left the store, after having touched the off and on switches to every stereo unit in the place, we took an elevator up one level. As we walked and talked, I began to feel a little better about my situation. Particularly Randy made me feel that mashing Ms. Velchur's carnation was an act of valor roughly on a par with the invasion of Normandy. If only Mantis had been in the store, I told him, I would have mashed her face.

As we reached the next elevator to go up yet another level, I saw a man on that level walking toward us. It took me only a second to recognize the figure of a man I had so often followed. The images of the next few seconds swept by me fast and furious. Randy and Lawrence Papsun, D.D.S., in the same place at the same time, each not knowing that I knew the other.

As it had on so many occasions before, my Traveling Pain came to my rescue by hurling a knife blow to my abdomen of sufficient force to make me keel over.

"My God," said Randy, reaching over to help. Luckily, we were not yet in earshot or the apparent sight line of Lawrence.

"It must have been something I had for dinner," I gasped. "I've got to go. Let me go."

"You're not well, you can't go alone. Let me help you." Randy was really turning out to be a good friend. I felt his hands on my shoulders, trying to steady me.

I pulled away.

"This happens sometimes. It's just my stomach. I just need a restroom and then a good long rest at home. Just let me go."

"But I wanted you to meet someone. Chip." I turned to face Randy as he spoke. "He keeps his office open late on Thursdays and I wanted him to meet you."

I must have looked surprised. Randy looked as if I looked terribly surprised. "You told him about — about me?"

"No, I just wanted him to meet you as a friend from my exercise class. Like we met by accident. You know. . . ." He was rubbing his forehead, whether from worry about my health or about my big mouth, I don't know. But at this second, Lawrence must have recognized Randy, because I heard him call his name. A bit questioningly.

I was still bent over, in shadow. My face was still hidden from above.

"Well, now just tell him that some stranger got sick at the mall and you helped him to the restroom, OK? I'll meet him some other time."

"But are you going to be OK?"

"Yeah. Sure. It happens to me all the time."

And I ran like a thief, like a bandit, like Errol Flynn in a pirate movie, off into the night.

Early the next morning, after having been awake almost all of the night before, I made a major decision. My appointment with Lawrence that afternoon needed to be some sort of turning point. Of some sort. I mean, the night before had to have been some kind of warning from whatever forces in the universe that were still on my side.

There had to be some coherent reason why last night happened last night, just before this morning, right?

So I dressed very carefully, starching almost every bit of cloth that would be visible. And scrubbing every square inch of flesh on my body, so that Chip and I could meet each other as equals.

By now we spoke as equals, greeting each other with our first names as we both looked at the moon.

"Good afternoon, Wyatt," Chip said in his wonderful rumble of a voice.

"Hi, Chip," I answered. And he swung the chair around to have his final look at my teeth. By now, we'd done everything but bob the suckers, so he was just having this look in order to see that everything was in order. He was finished in minutes.

"Well, you look great," he said. "Inside and out. Is this a new suit?" he asked, fingering the lapel of my best Armani.

"No, I just don't get a chance to wear it all that often. I thought if I dressed right, you might accept my offer of a drink after we were done here. I am your last appointment of the day, right?"

"Well, yes. . . ."

I moved the tray of dental instruments out of the space between us. "Then there's no reason why we shouldn't take a few minutes and get to know each other better."

We were quiet for a moment while I breathed in the clean sweet smells of his body. I ran my fingertip from the high top of his forehead down the ridge of his nose and across his lips.

"Now just a moment — " he started.

"It's all right," I calmed him, running my finger across his lips. "I know. I know all about you. And, believe me, it's just fine with me."

I knew this was the moment. This was when all the events would just start their spinning, or they wouldn't. I knew from all those past experiences, that no matter how attracted you might be to someone, if nothing happens in a set short period of time, it never will. And I knew that I knew that I wanted something to happen here, no matter what it did to Randy or to Chip or to me or to anyone else. I wanted to fling this man in this chair and turn this chair around and make it with the man in the moon.

I pulled our heads closer, my hand on the back of his neck. I swear that my skin burned at the touch of his flesh. I swear that the clocks stopped ticking, the phones stopped ringing and time just stood still.

It was as if I were kissing someone else for the very first time. As if my lips had never met another pair of lips, had never parted those lips and moved within the basin of breath. It was more than affection, more than lust, it was the complete joining of two bodies, two souls. I could feel our hearts begin to beat with one rhythm, our breath becoming as one self-sustaining cycle, the carbon dioxide he expelled became oxygen in my lungs. Our two bodies were growing together for all time.

And then the asshole, the chump, the jerk pulled away.

A current of electricity flew through me with the same jolt as house current. He pulled away, broke the connection, a look of shock, and also of arousal in his eyes.

"What the hell do you think you're doing?" he asked in his strong man's voice. The words growled out of his vocal cords.

"Trying to show you how clean my teeth are?" All right, it was a weak attempt at a joke, but for a moment, I began to think that Randy was dating some other guy named Chip.

Although he didn't laugh, or do anything even remotely like laughing, Chip softened a bit. He sat back down in the chair he'd jumped out of only moments before.

"Hey, look, I'm flattered," he began, "but I'm just not interested."

"Not interested?" I asked. "In men?"

At this question, his face reddened. I could watch the rush of embarrassment push from his forehead down to where his neck disappeared into his collar.

"No," he said evenly, honestly. "I am interested in men."

"Well? Then what?"

"I am not interested in you."

Now this, and I know I was a jerk not to have considered it, never occurred to me. In my life, I have never allowed myself to not be interested in any person — OK, any man — who had been interested in me. Kinsey report not withstanding, I haven't found in this lifetime enough men interested in outies and not innies for me to feel that I could be choosy. And I looked at his starched clean clean being and I lusted for it, and more, I was sure that I loved it.

But he just wasn't having any.

"I'm sorry," he said. His voice was pitched a little higher this time.

"You're sorry? I'm sorry for making assumptions. For putting you on a spot like this."

"No, really, I'm the one who is sorry. It's just that I am sort of a little involved, you know. Nothing really serious or permanent or anything — I mean, we don't live together — but I feel sort of awkward about this whole thing."

"Hey, I understand. I'm sorry for pushing it. I just find you really attractive. . . ."

And I put my hand down lightly over his hand, rubbing my thumb over his knuckle.

"You know, it's just not a good time for me right now," he started to say, but by then, I had pushed our heads together and we were kissing again.

And again, it was lightning and thunder and all the natural displays of the power of the universe. It was all the gravity and energy flow available. It was the tornado in *The Wizard of Oz*. And like that tornado, it ended with a house being dropped.

This time he got angry. This time he shoved me back

in the chair and held me there with his overdeveloped forearms.

"Now you fucking cut this out!" he was trying to show me that there was no doubt in his mind. But what he was showing me was that there was nothing BUT doubt in his mind. He was showing me with this sole display of thunder and lightning that he had felt the energy that we cooked up together. He was showing me the power he held in his own two good arms.

"OKAY. Okay." I said, and he lowered his arms. "I won't try it again." He backed away slowly.

"I better go now," I said as I began to slowly get up from the chair. He stood, sagging a bit, just a couple of feet away. As I stood I could see that he was just an inch or two taller than I was, just a short reach above me, just as I like them. And I had finally had a chance to feel his body, his sinewy strength, I wanted to be running my fingernails down his bare back, while he made me come and come and come.

I straightened the lapels of the suit and smoothed out everything that had been rumpled.

I looked over at his face. His eyes were narrowed. His nostrils flared like a horse that had just completed a gallop. His skin was reddened now in every visible place. I saw confusion on his face. And anger. And then I saw what I needed to see, what I'd been searching for, needing to find — I saw longing.

I walked over to the office door, slowly. Vowing that I wouldn't trouble him again. That I would simply (ha ha) pay my bill, thank him for his time and then find a new dentist.

But when I reached the door, instead of turning the knob, I locked it. I moved my body around, catlike, and faced this man that I wanted, that I needed to see ache and bleed and long for me. And lifted my hands from the doorknob, and move them with my arms with a grace that would woo Bruce Lee, and flowingly, lovingly I spread my legs and brought my tongue to my lips and my arms to my hips, letting him see me gloriously akimbo.

That was when we went together to the moon.

40

There is a crystal sheen over the city of Atlanta. Although the air is as warm as it would be in any springtime, there is a chill that pierces itself into your bones.

Yankees.

The word is everywhere, hissed.

In the ragged months since the War Between the States began, our Southern gentlemen have faced setback after setback. And now, that Yankee Devil, General Orly Kasaba, was using his fierce forces to burn a hole in the heart of Dixie. As he moved, he kept on calling out his goal — to drive all the way to the sea, a path that would bring him through Atlanta.

The city steeled itself. The once graceful population center now prided itself on armaments. Shutters covered every window. Black wreaths were nailed on every door.

The hospitals were crowded beyond their capacity. It was there, where I was working my shift, praying with some, cutting the arms and legs off others, that my little slave boy Benny found me.

"Massa Wildroot!" I heard him scream in his nasal uneducated and completely uncultured voice.

"Over here, Benny," I said, still moving among the sick and wounded, giving morphine here, just touching a dampened forehead there. I had been working now for some thirty hours straight, although the doctor had told me I must look to my own health. But I knew that as long as I had strength in my own body, I would be here helping these brave soldiers.

"It Miss Pixie," Benny shrieked. "Her time has come."

Miss Pixie was the whitewash girl that I had taken into my home, despite the dangers she presented to us all, in that she had been impregnated by a Yankee soldier and had, in fact, slept with the majority of those who made up the Union forces. But no matter, her child was innocent, and if that child, born in wartime, could live and grow, he would grow up strong and beautiful and free. That is what we were all living and fighting for.

"I'm coming, Benny," I called as I rolled down the white cotton sleeves of my shirt and grabbed my black cotton blend coat. And, as we ran, we ran through the center square of the town, the place in which we had to leave our growing numbers of wounded out to dry in the sun, before we could see to their arms and legs. As I threaded through the huge mass of suffering, I felt as if my spirit were pulling free of my body, rising higher and higher, seeing more and more of the crowd, as if I were swinging higher and higher in my perception. And I could hear "Dixie" playing, I was sure, soft and slow. And my eyes were high above us now, in an atmosphere dominated by the sight of a tattered Confederate flag.

It was Benny's clawed grasp on my arm that pulled me back to reality and we ran through the street, hurried to the little stone mansion that we called home.

"Massa Wildroot," Benny called over his shoulder. "Miss Pixie has been callin' and callin' for you somethin' fierce, but you done tol' me not to come and get you until

it was her time, so I done waited just like you tol' me, until I was sure, then I come get you right away, just like you tol' me to yourself."

I tapped Benny lightly on the back of the shoulders with my fist, this being the only way to quiet him when he went on so. We flew up the sidewalk of my house.

Inside, in the dreadful Southern heat, Pixie lay, great with child. Her face smudged with a dab of dirt, as were the faces of all White Trash.

"How are you feeling?" I asked Miss Pixie as I stroked her hand.

"I think I'm going to DIIIEEEEE!" shrieked my Pixie as she reached up at blank shadows on the ceiling.

I knew immediately that this was beyond the grasp of medicine, as hand holding hadn't worked and there was nothing here to amputate. Luckily, Benny had already set my mind at rest by telling me that he knew everything about the birth process, having assisted at the birth of many fine Southern children.

I called him out of the room, to the landing of the stairs. "Now, Benny," I began. "It's Miss Pixie's time and you were just right in coming to get me. But now you must go in there and deliver that baby."

"What baby?" asked Benny.

"Miss Pixie's baby."

"She gonna have a baby?"

It was then that I first hit Benny, a solid blow. "You said you could help her, that you knew just what to do."

"I thought she was just having female trouble," Benny said, hopping on one leg like a child who needs to urinate.

"Get in there and help her," I ordered him.

"But I don't know nothing 'bout birthin' babies!" Benny shrieked, rolling his eyes in their sockets.

I knew that there was no more time to be wasted with his nonsense and pushed him down the stairs. "Get in that kitchen and boil water, and plenty of it," I called to him below.

I will not move again through the details of what happened next, except to say that my unwavering faith guided me through and it was not until I cut the cord with my teeth that I knew I had done a fine job bringing the child into the world.

But it was then that I heard the first shot, the sound of Kasaba's march on Atlanta. And I knew that our troubles had just begun, that these were dangers greater than childbirth.

I stood at the top of the long staircase, wondering what to do, where to turn for help in this city on the verge of destruction.

And then I knew that there was just one man who could be trusted, who had the virility and strength to save us all — to get us all through. And that was Captain Lawrence Papsun, D.D.S.

"Wildroot," Captain Papsun growled at the air when he saw me enter the old stable where the Yankees were holding him prisoner. Having had nothing else to wear, I had forced Benny to sew me a new suit from the one fine piece of material that we still owned — my mother's velvet curtains. The result, shaped from an old Italian suit of mine used as a pattern, was a surprisingly supple and clinging green velvet day suit, of unbelievable heat in the Southern sun. But I looked good.

The Yankee soldiers, moved by the passion that flowed between my captain and myself, allowed us a brief moment of privacy. As we embraced and I kissed his whiskey-soaked mouth, I pulled a small knife from my vest pocket and slipped it into his groping hands.

Before I had even cleared the stable doors as I made my exit, I could hear the sounds of the struggle as Captain Papsun freed himself.

Seemingly moments later, we were flying free on the top of a Yankee cart, pulled by a fine team of horses. "Oh, Wildroot, Wildroot, Wildroot, I have missed you so. Let's get out of this dying place."

And he pulled the reins to force the horses to leap through a blazing wall, as the Yankees, while we were sewing the suit, had broken into Atlanta.

I wanted to tell him that we must hurry and get Miss Pixie and her baby and my faithful servant, Benny. I wanted to grab the reins and turn us around. But then I looked at the strong profile of Captain Lawrence Papsun, D.D.S., set off against the fires in the night. And I reached my hand into his torn and tattered shirt, pinching a nipple lightly.

"Yes, let's. Let's drive and drive until we find a place that is without war, and then let's lay down in the grass and love each other wildly," I shouted out into the night, my lips moist against his neck.

And he grabbed me by the waist and pulled me next to him, and we drove. We drove off into the night.

41

After that Chip didn't even get mad at me when I told him I had no job and no medical plan and no money to pay my bill.

And we hadn't yet — how to put this? — consummated the relationship.

In fact, as I lay with my face resting in his damp fur,

I can remember having had the sensation of disappoint-ment, in that he had shot out so quickly, almost as quickly as I de-smocked the man. As I saw his winter-white body, with its fine blond hairs, spread-eagled in the dental chair facing the moon graphic.

In fact, the force of his eruption erased several of the moon's craters.

He slumped back immediately, looking ready for a long sleep, while I curled up and put my nose to work breathing in his muskiness. Memorizing his scent.

I had figured the whole thing out — how it should all go. We could use one finger cut from a dental glove as a rubber and take our lubrication from any of the several flouride gels, even have choice of flavor. But this was not to be, leaving things, as I say, unconsummated.

But, as soon as Lawrence was fully alert again, I detailed my plan out to him, evoking some, if not quite enough, interest on his part. The old spirit was willing but the flesh was weak. Or limp, rather. So we decided to forego any more attempts for that evening and try again. Real soon.

But, since that time, we have had to return from our moun-taintop experience. And, although I can still evoke his scent to fill my heart with animal lust, the most we've managed is a quick lunch and an after-work drink.

I appreciate the fact that Lawrence lives in fear of Randy walking into any restaurant we might inhabit. In fact, I encourage Lawrence to talk to me all he wants about his relationship with Randy. And I am encouraged by the result of the conversations. It's the standard theme — Lawrence feels misunderstood by Randy and underappreciated in love. What's worse, Randy appears to be the proof of the axiom — "It's not the meat, it's the motion" — in that, with all that fine meat, he seems not to be able to do much with it.

I have grown used to seeing Lawrence across the table from me, a whiskey in his hand. I feel I could see that face and that hand every day for the rest of my life and never tire of them.

I have to admit here that there is something so wonderfully mysterious to me about men, about their existence, their cocks, that when I find that each new man has a cock standing out hard between his legs, I am surprised anew by this miracle. It never seems to be standard equipment, somehow. I just want to marvel at what swings between the legs.

And most men get embarrassed, for some strange stupid reason. But not Lawrence Papsun, D.D.S. He revels in the attention and has taken to giving me late afternoon appointments two or three times a week and working on my teeth (he still cannot just call it an appointment and close and lock the door for fun and laughs; he has to perform actual dental work if he is calling it a dental appointment) while naked from the waist down.

And it makes me delirious to feel his hard organ press against me, burning hot, while he probes my mouth with his hands.

While my bill is now well over $2,000, Lawrence tells me not to worry. That he'll give me the money, to pay the bills himself if need be, but that I must never never, for the sake of my dental health, miss an appointment.

But still and all, with all the tease, and with all the sleek swift showing and feeling and smelling of hair and muscle, we have not consummated the relationship.

And worse, I have not taken any time to find a new job, or any source of money, as my time is taken up either visiting my nude dentist or by jerking off remembering what it was like having his hard cock touch me all over my body.

I go home every night to one less can of tuna as I make my dinner. I look each morning at my checkbook to find it to contain just a little less money.

And yet, I cannot work myself into misery over this. In that I am sure that I will die of frustration long before I can ever starve to death.

42

February 27

Dear Diary,

I knew the moment I opened my eyes that this would be the blackest of days. A Tuesday. As I faced the morning from inside my apartment window, I saw that it was one of those late winter mornings, those that hover around the freezing point.

The television agreed with my appraisal of the day. We would have snow mixing with and then turning into rain, which would freeze into sleet before changing back into snow again around sunset.

And I wouldn't have chosen this day to go out into the world, except for two reasons: (1) this was the morning that Unemployment had set for my hearing to see whether or not I was due any money from them because I got fired and not laid off, and they were, I had quickly gathered, not the sort of people that you could call and say that you didn't want to come down this morning because you didn't want to drive in snow; and (2) I was totally out of tuna and would have to use what little cash I had left to buy some more food to last me until my unemployment checks started and I had some money again.

So I got up and found, upon getting into my shower, that there was very little hot water in my very cold little apartment. Not that I was going to complain to the landlord about either situation, in that I had not yet paid the total amount of rent for the month of February, although I had paid some, and I had no idea where the March rent was coming from, in that Unemployment, even IF I got it, would not cover both rent and the rest of my monthly expenses — food, gas, electric, etc. — giving me the choice of heat and light but no apartment or an apartment but no heat and light.

But that was tomorrow's dilemma in that I didn't have any Unemployment rights as yet until after my hearing this morning.

So I got ready as best as I could, given the heat and hot water situation and, of course, I wore my black Armani and freshly ironed and starched white cotton shirt. I chose a sedate tie with just a touch of red in it. And wore my black dress shoes that were made of a smooth black leather, so soft and cunning that they were just a millimeter above glove leather for protection. I usually only wore them with my tuxedo, which I held ever at the ready, but I thought that I needed them today. I wanted to portray myself as the wounded professional person up against the savage corporation, as represented in Ms. Velchur, sort of David versus Goliath.

In my first appointment with Unemployment, a large black woman named Carole was very nice to me. Which she should have been, as I waited over an hour in a long long line just to get the chance to visit with her. She showed me which forms to fill out and what to write on them. And then pointed me over to a table to do my work. And an hour later, after again waiting in the line, I got back to the front and handed in my papers. That's when she told me that there

would have to be a hearing, in that the store said I was
rightfully fired and I claimed that a personality conflict was
the trigger to the whole thing, and that I had always ful-
filled my job professionally and well.

Carole told me not to worry about the hearing, in that
they were pretty much just a formality around the office
and that Unemployment always stacked the chips in favor
of the employee, no matter how scummy they were.

And a quick glance around the room attested to the fact
that they were scummy. I had never seen so many beer bellies
and unshaved faces and legs and armpits in one room before.

So I pretty much went out the door to my appointment
still trying to decide how to spend the money — on food
or on shelter. Which was a true conundrum, in that I could
no longer ask Randy for money — in fact, I had quit Arlene's
Sweat It Out for good this time, so that I would never have
to face Randy with the knowledge of what I'd done to him,
and had never returned the phone messages he'd left on my
machine — since I had stolen his boyfriend, who was now
my new boyfriend, sort of replacing Randy himself. And
Lawrence Papsun, D.D.S., being a D.D.S. had tons of money
as far as I knew — he certainly has a new car and a wonderful looking apartment/condo (I don't know which or what
it was, or what it looked like on the inside, as Lawrence
lived in fear that if I went inside we would find Randy had
used his key and was waiting there for us). But Lawrence
seems not willing or able to deal with my troubles, and has
never once mentioned anything to do with money, except
that I shouldn't worry about the dental bills which I still
continue to receive almost daily in the mail.

So, I went out into the elements.

The first thing I had to do, naturally, this being February,
the longest shortest month in history, was scrape all the new

snow and ice off my car, just to keep up with all the new snow and ice that was coming down.

In doing this, I managed to do two things: (1) to totally cover the front of my one good cashmere overcoat with thick snow, that also covered my head and face, getting my hair — that I had carefully styled to hide the fact that it hadn't been cut for weeks — all wet and leaving me freezing and shivering; and (2) filling my shoes with snow that melted instantly to water, ruining these foxy leather pumps.

So, the first step to hell.

Then I got into the car and tried to turn over the engine. It sounded vaguely feline, a bit of a growl, as it refused to turn over. So I knew that I should have started the engine every day in winter but I had been depressed and hadn't. So what?

I went back into the apartment and called AAA, who told me that they would be happy to rush right over and jump-start my car, but that it would take at least an hour. I tried to explain that I was due downtown in a half hour, but that did little good. They just wanted my card number, and, when I gave that to them, told me that my card had expired and that I should have a good day.

I ran back to the parking lot and tried the car again. This time, the engine didn't even try to turn over. Since it was after nine A.M. by now, the only other car in the whole lot was Mrs. Abernathy's blue Pacer. She was the only one in the whole building, aside from myself, who wasn't working, and she was a retired widow on a fixed income.

I risked angering her and tapped on her door. Mrs. Abernathy had never liked me much since she figured out that she could not bother trying to fix me up with one of her nieces. In fact, she once made quite a fuss when she saw me walking in the door with an especially cute guy I'd met at a party. I guess we'd been a little too obvious in front of Mrs. Abernathy, who was of the old school — that you should, if you *have* to do these sort of depraved things, hide them from the general public.

But I should have known that I could count on Mrs. Abernathy when the chips were down. Being of my mother's age and generation, it came as sort of a knee-jerk reaction to her to mother anyone of a younger generation who found himself in need. Which I was — very much in need.

Her apartment had the old person's smell, which I could detect the moment she opened the door a crack to see who it was. She only had to look at my face and, like my mother, she started the conversation with, "What's the matter?"

I told her my story, as I dripped on her welcome mat. Mrs. Abernathy responded with professional motherhood. She threw a coat on over her robe and a scarf on over her curlers and we ran out the front door. I lied to her to the extent that I told her I had a job interview, instead of one with Unemployment. This was like school to any mother, a place that you HAD TO GET TO and on time. After all, I figured that everyone in the building knew by now that I was out of work, since this was one of those buildings in which people kept an eye out for such things as cars that stay in the parking lot too late in the day. Mrs. Abernathy confirmed this — that there had been talk in the laundry room about my situation.

Her Pacer, an old wreck like mine, started right up. "You have to come out and start the engine every day, whether or not you're going somewhere," she told me as she ran the cables from her battery to mine and then jump-started my car. "Don't turn it off now for twenty minutes or so, so that it can recharge," she told me and then ran back into the apartment house, wishing me luck.

I drove downtown and arrived about fifteen minutes late for my hearing, which to me seemed like a miracle.

But on my way into the Unemployment building, I was knocked down the second step toward destruction. For, as

I managed to sort of parallel park my car, something I've never been any too good at, I grabbed the handful of papers that I needed for the meeting and ran to the office door. On the way, I hit a patch of ice and found myself sliding then toppling and then falling on the pavement, which, mirabile dictu, left me uninjured. As I rose to my feet I was amazed that I wasn't hurt, just shaken, and began, for a moment, to believe that the day might get better. It didn't. For I looked down at my knee and saw the rip in my Armani trousers that I'd bought as part of this smart business suit when I still had a store discount, which I no longer had, even if I had the money to buy a new suit.

So by now, I was pretty disheartened, right?

But worse was to come, most especially when I realized very quickly that Carole, my lovely friend, would not be taking my hearing, but that Mr. Swipe, the bald man with deep creases around his eyes — and not laugh lines, but frown lines — and very thick glasses would be taking my case from here.

The first thing Mr. Swipe did was point out that I was late. And I believe that it was only the torn pants, my soggy hair and my ruined shoes that kept me from being dismissed right then and there.

Which he might as well have done, in that Mr. Swipe had no intention of giving me any of my Unemployment rights. In that he had a sworn statement from Ms. Velchur that had listed my crimes against the store and against humanity. And I believe that it was the arriving drunk at seven P.M. with a collection of greasy paper plates that had done me in with Mr. Swipe, just as it had with Ms. Velchur. Within moments, Mr. Swipe had shot holes right through my "personality conflict" argument, and made me feel that I was lucky to be getting away without a prison term.

Which maybe I was.

So I went back out to my car, which, of course, had a

ticket on it, in that I hadn't taken the time to put money in the meter.

Then I drove down to my bank, where I thought, what the hell? and closed out my account. With the $42 that gave me, I figured I had two choices: (1) I could buy enough food to last me one more week, by which time I'd most likely be thrown out into the streets; or (2) I could buy a gun and rob old ladies like Mrs. Abernathy and then shoot myself when the police caught up with me.

I went with the first choice and bought $38 dollars worth of tuna and a *TV Guide*.

Then I drove to the mall.

I had decided somewhere in the grocery store that I should confront Mantis with her crimes against both me and humanity.

When I got to the store, I had been windblown some more and looked even worse, if such a thing were possible. I avoided the area of the beauty salon out of fear that Tommy or one of the other boys would see me and invite me into the shop for a free cut and cup of coffee out of pity. I feared this in that I knew I would take them up on their free offer and then spill the whole story, which would be all over the store in minutes and all over town in an hour.

I went back to my old office to find that it had been painted ice white and that everything had a place and was in that place. And, worse, each place was marked with a graphic — stenciled letters that said, "pens," and "wire," and "flowers, dried." Like that.

Well, Mantis wasn't in my — I mean, her — office. Someone that I'd never seen before who was working ladies wear right outside the office said that she was at lunch and I could find her in the company cafeteria.

Without my badge, that wasn't an easy place to crash.

But I found that I still had one friend in Lucille, the hen-
naed number who sat by the cafeteria door checking badges.
She either liked me, or was stupid enough to buy the story
that I was meeting my dear friend Mantis here for lunch.
I no longer cared which.

I saw Mantis immediately. And she saw me. Across the
proverbial crowded room. I was damned happy to see that
she was sitting alone, proving to me that no one liked her
any more than I did.

When Mantis saw me, she began to rise slightly from
her dish of lime Jello. Then she sat again. Then rose again
and sat, like a trapped animal. Like a deer in the headlights.
She knew that her number was up.

I crossed that cafeteria like Marshall Dillon. I no longer
cared that she was right smack in the center of the room
and that anything that we said or did to each other would
be luncheon fodder for weeks.

"Fauna said that this one should not talk to you," Mantis
said as I sat across from her at the table.

"Fauna's not here now," I retorted and a pretty good
retort it was, although I wished that the Fauna bitch were
here right now and that she had her bronze doorknocker
with her so that I could shove that goddamned doorknocker
up her goddamned ass.

"And cut the talking about yourself in the third person,
like goddamned baby talk," I continued. By now I was very
angry, which is when I say "goddamned" a lot.

"Fauna says you owe her money," said Mantis evenly.
She was a cool number.

"What's that to you?" I retorted. Again, a good retort.
"Why do you keep bringing up Fauna — what is she, your
lover?"

I don't know why these words came out of my mouth,
but I knew the moment I'd said them, even before looking
to see her reaction, that I'd been right. Fauna and Mantis

were lovers, which would be why Fauna would work so hard to get Mantis a job — my job.

Now this changed things a bit, and made it a little harder to hate Mantis. Now she was a political "sister," in that she faced the same hatreds and prejudices that I had had to face and struggle with all my life. Suddenly she looked like a very young, very stupid little girl from Texas who was doing her best to prove herself to herself and that overbearing bitch Fauna, who, no doubt, had been running the whole show from the background. And the fact that Mantis, in her way, WAS a very talented display artist made it both more and less difficult for me to hate her.

I was puzzled as to what to do next. But this puzzlement as to whether or not to kill the woman — and I did wish that I'd gone ahead and bought the gun, although I could have killed her with a can of tuna if I'd beaten her over the head with it, didn't stop me from smashing her lime Jello in her face and calling her "Lesbian Freak Bitch" at the top of my lungs in the middle of the cafeteria. After all, I felt I owed these people a show and I intended to give them one.

I stalked out of the cafeteria to scattered applause.

Fauna was next.

And I was right when I figured that Mantis would get on the phone and call her.

"You owe me $50," was all she said to me when she opened her door after I'd pounded down on the knocker.

"You owe me a lot more than that, you cunt bitch," I yelled at her. See, I was really really angry by now, way past "goddamned."

"Shut your mouth," she said, and slapped me. Hard.

And suddenly, like Tippie Hedren in *Marnie,* all I saw was red.

And it was the annual Alexis/Krystle duel to the death. I leaped on her like a jungle tiger. She swatted at me with her lion's paws. And we rolled on the Oriental rug like crazed animals, each trying to rip the other's throat out with bare teeth.

I don't know how long we fought like this. I do remember the crash of furniture, the sound of gasps and shrieks and the crunch of bones. And I do remember that several of those bones were mine and that I was bleeding and that Fauna and I were evenly matched.

In the end, it was exhaustion that won. As we rolled off one another and turned over on our backs on the Oriental rug, we laid our arms across our faces and puffed for a bit, trying to regain our breath. Then, when I could stand, I walked out her front doorway, slamming the door hard enough to bring the knocker crashing down on the floor below. With a large wet thud.

Then I went out and had a car accident.

What else could I do at this point?

I moved to my car as best as I could, realizing too late that I'd thrown off my overcoat as I'd lept at Fauna. And that it had my last four dollars in the pocket. But no way was I going back there now.

And broken, bleeding, and alone, I got into my Datsun and started the engine. I remember again thinking it a miracle that something went right, that my car started, only to find out later that it would have been so much kinder if instead it had refused to turn over. But, at that moment, I just wanted out of there before the police arrived, since I would have to hurl cans of tuna at them to hold them at bay.

And I drove off into a premature sunset that was made up of thicker and thicker cloud cover that still poured forth snow/rain/sleet.

And, of course, I drove too fast. Not a little too fast. A lot too fast. And before I'd gone through too many traffic lights, I managed to hit a Toyota that was coming in the opposite direction minding its own business.

At least I could blame the car wreck on the way I looked. When the police came, they assured me that the driver of the car I'd hit was fine, and then issued me with a whopper of a ticket. They also took a look at me and tried to get me to go to the hospital. But there was one more place I had to go that day. One more thing I could do, and then I could die happy.

I exchanged insurance information with the other driver and with the police, thanking God that I had at least not let that expire. Then I sent my car on to a repair shop with a tow truck, whose driver I paid with a check on a bank account that no longer existed. I figured that I'd be dead before he could come looking for me.

And then, quite suddenly, really, I was standing all alone in the dark and the snow. I marveled for a moment that none of them seemed to care that they were leaving a tattered and bloody man standing alone in the dark and the cold and the snow.

And for a moment I just stood there, amazed at the quiet of the snow-covered city. And amazed that that quiet had filled me also. I then began to walk, quite calmly, to my destination.

I don't know how long I walked. My watch had been smashed in the car wreck. But I neither felt the cold of having wet shoes and no overcoat, nor did I feel hunger. It wasn't until much later that I realized that all my tuna had been towed away with my auto.

But I walked with a purpose, bent over against the snow. Slowly, steadily, like the tortoise instead of the hare. For the first time, not the hare.

I walked to my destination with a purpose. And the few

people who were still on the streets moved out of my way to let me pass.

And then, the last few blocks, the last three or four, I ran and ran full tilt. I'd found more power in myself today than I'd ever before known I could have.

And, at last, I stood before her building and called her name out loud and clear. Like Stanley does Stella. Like a wolf bays at the moon. Only here could anyone save me. Only here would I find help.

And I called out her name again, like a child calls "Mommy," when trapped within an awful dream.

And I gasped with relief when I saw the light in the window as she parted her shades.

And I knew that she would help me now, but I just kept on calling and calling her name, this being the only thing still within my strength to keep doing. And I called and kept on calling, "Dina, Dina, Dina!"

43

I remember her hand chucking me under my chin and one tear drifting out of my eye.

And then everything seemed all right again.

I was sitting by the fireplace at the far end of the room. I was wrapped in a blanket, and held a mug of hot herbal tea in my hand. I was barefoot. And I vibrated internally as the anxiety slowly drained from my body.

"Do you want to talk about it yet?" Dina asked me.

In all the time that it took for her to get me from her

stoop and into her home, she never quizzed me. Not as she told me to take off my wet clothes and left me in a room to do so. Not as she opened the door to that room slowly, and just enough to reach in with a warm soft bathrobe. And not as she threw the blanket over my shoulders and led me to the fire that she had built to warm me.

I had expected the herbal tea. Everything else was a lovely surprise.

"No, I don't want to talk yet," I answered.

And so we continued as we had been. Dina moved about the room as she must have been doing before she heard me in the snow. She moved efficiently and quietly, working at some project.

She would rise and get a book and then return to her desk and open that book, find the passage she sought, and then write something on the paper in front of her. Or she would reach for a file and open it, again copying some important part.

She worked although she surely knew that I stared. She never looked up, never challenged me with her gaze, but just kept working, knowing that I would talk when ready.

And, to my eyes, she shimmered and changed, as she'd always done, from her own self to Madame Curie bent over some lifesaving experiment to Eleanor Roosevelt, busy traveling around a broken America, being her husband's legs.

"You are so good to me." I said finally.

And then it became so easy to talk. And Dina came and sat again by my side and I told her the whole story. All of it. The images of things that I had had and how those images were changed. And how I'd lost my job and my money and my possibility of a life tomorrow. And now she didn't take any notes, didn't interrupt me with a word or even a sigh, but she just listened. And, as I poured out my story, I felt as if I were pouring it into her, as if she were a vase I was filling.

And all the while, although I looked mostly at the fire, I could feel her eyes on me, burning as warmly as the fire. And I knew that this place, with her office in the front and her home in the rear, was, and always had been, my home also. That, if Lawrence had asked to see where I lived, if I had decided to show him where I truly lived, I would have driven him past Dina's.

I think that we talked for hours that night, as she slowly drew forth my entire story, my entire litany of fear and guilt.

And never once did she ask me what I intended to do tomorrow. Somewhere in there, however, she brought me hot soup and homemade bread and I ate while still talking.

And I felt as the hours passed that I was growing lighter. As if weights were being lifted from my shoulders.

And it was not for several hours that it even occurred to me to ask her why this man's robe was in her home, and even then I decided that that was a question that could be asked tomorrow. Like the question of Benny.

Because now I knew that there would be a tomorrow for me and for Dina and for the two of us together. Because in her, I knew at last, I had more than a doctor, and more than a shifting image of woman — from Amazon to scientist — I had a true friend.

44

It wasn't until the morning, after I'd drifted off to sleep on the couch, watching the fire fade as did my consciousness, that we got around to basics.

Dina had, I found out in the morning, called to make sure of Fauna's health somewhere during my sleep. Fauna would not, Dina assured me, press any charges and was chalking the whole thing up to Karma. She, of course, believed that our little episode would heap hot coals over my head, as I believed she was heaping them over hers.

It wasn't until morning that I finally asked about the robe. I felt that I was being very kind and friend-like to wait until morning. Dina seemed to find it an invasion at any time. Not that she said anything directly to that extent. She just looked at me across the table in her breakfast nook, where I was eating cinnamon rolls and drinking more herbal tea, and said, "Then I suppose you don't want to borrow any of his street clothes."

Well, this indeed did shut me up on the subject, as I was very much in need of borrowing something in the way of business or sportswear to get myself safely back to the apartment.

But the issues got more and more difficult and my actions more obtuse.

The subject of Benny came up next. And, as I suspected, I finally forced Dina to admit to having been seeing Benny behind my back. She even admitted that she found nothing wrong with this — just because it was her job — and told me that she had never spoken to me about Benny's sessions because he had asked her not to. As if she should have respected his right to privacy over my need to know.

But, as the morning wore on, and most especially after I heard Dina call and reschedule another patient so that she could spend more time with me, I began to admit grudgingly that maybe she could have been doing Benny some good, and that, just because I insisted on telling all the people I knew about my therapy sessions, maybe it was all right for Benny to seek help in secret.

And on the subject of the bathrobe, she was absolutely not to be swayed. I even believe that she punished me a bit for even bringing it up in that she appeared from her bedroom closet with a jogging suit for me to wear home. A powder blue jogging suit.

When I began to raise my voice in comment, she said, "Don't let's get back on a bad foot, OK?"

And it was the plaintive "OK" that really wore me down. After all, this was the woman who'd rescued me from the snow. Who'd fed me and clothed me and seen to it that Fauna would not have me arrested for assault. If this woman were great with child and riding on a donkey, there would have been no room in the inn for her in my opinion, if you get my meaning.

The woman had a halo.

But then we got on to the hardest topic of all. Lawrence Papsun, D.D.S.

Here, too, Dina was adamant. And it crossed my mind that this was less therapy than it was taking a badly behaved child by the hand and showing him how he should act. And I was putting up with it. Hell, I knew that it was nothing less than I deserved.

Dina broke the issue down into subtopics: (1) there was the story of Randy, who, despite the appellation pig-dog had turned out to be an OK Joe, and maybe even better than that. In fact he had turned out to be a very nice person who deserved better than the pain I was willing to cause him; and (2) there was the problem with Lawrence Papsun, D.D.S., himself. The problem with the fact that he seemed to downplay and actually downright ignore his own seeming lack of ability to commit. How he was so willing to sell his relationship with Randy right down the river when the opportunity came for him to do his dental work while naked from the waist down. And how he apparently had not offered me anything in the way of a real relationship, and had only so far disappointed me in terms of sex.

Both were good points, I had to admit.

Dina said that she felt that it was time for me to take my life into my own hands if I were ever going to bother to do so. And that that meant I had to look at the situation dead-on, and not color it with the shades that I wanted. And that it might mean that I had to just get out of Randy and Lawrence's lives, because it sounded like they had a few things to work out on their own.

More good points, I had to admit.

And then I had to notice that I had never heard Dina speak so many words at one time before. And had never seen her be so passionate.

It was like she was worried about me or something.

So, by noon I had promised Dina that I would step back from the whole Randy/Lawrence situation and that I would take a look at that situation from a distance, objectively. This meant that I shouldn't see or talk to either of them for at least a week. Seemed simple to me.

And then she praised me for one little thing — for having at last told Pixie about me and Rollo. Although she said that I now had to follow through and build a new relationship with Pixie, one built on faith and trust.

I asked if that meant that I had to tell her about Orly Kasaba. But she only looked at me. I already knew the answer.

Finally, Dina handed me $50. "I am only lending this to you, I want you to know," she said as she tucked it into the pocket of the jogging suit. "But don't hurry to pay it back. And I want you to come for a session every day for the next few weeks, just until you're back on your feet. And don't worry about my fee, we'll work something out."

And then she put me in her Volvo and drove me home. I waved at her from the apartment house doorway until she was out of sight.

It wasn't until I'd already changed my clothing and made sure that nothing in my little apartment had changed while I was gone that I noticed the blinking red light on my answering machine.

There were two calls. The first was Randy. "Wyatt," he said to the tape, "I was just checking on you. Please call me. Just to let me know if you need anything."

The second call was from Lawrence. "I need to see you right away," he said. And then he hung up.

Well, I was in that cab in minutes, Dina's loan in my pocket, ready to pay for the ride and whatever else I'd be expected to spring for.

I told Lawrence's nurse Nancy, with whom I was also on a first-name basis by now, that Lawrence had wanted to see me. "I think he just got my new X-rays back," I said, and the explanation, if she cared at all, seemed to satisfy her.

No sooner did Nancy buzz Lawrence than he opened his office door, and I was taken inside.

As soon as the door closed, Lawrence began to pace the room frantically and shout at me.

"Where were you last night?" he asked me with a sharp edge to his voice.

"I stayed at a friend's."

The answer seemed only to upset him more. He ran his hands through his hair like Heathcliffe.

"It's not what you think," I continued. "I got stuck at a FEMALE friend's house. I had a little traffic accident and she let me stay overnight."

His relief was palpable. He wheeled his little work chair around to face me. I expected him at any minute to drop his pants and start in working.

"Look," he said, and he took my hand. "I've been kind of confused about this relationship thing for a while now. But I want to give it a chance. When I called you up last night, and your machine answered, I just went crazy. I wanted to — had to see you."

All of this was coming out in little bursts of words. None of this was easy for Lawrence Papsun, D.D.S.

"Look," he continued. I was really starting to be a little entertained by all this, what with Dina's insights into Lawrence's character and all.

"Look, I want you to go away with me. Right now. Just pack your bags. I have the tickets. We fly to Florida and then get on a boat and sail away for a few days. I've already got the tickets and the traveler's checks and the cash and the whole thing. I want to give this a chance." He leaned closer. "Will you come with me?"

The thoughts that went around my head: better than a free meal, a free trip, out of the snow and the cold and away from my landlord and the tow truck driver who was going to be hearing from my bank any time now. A chance to run away with the man that I'd pursued like a crazy for months. But also with the man who was already involved with my friend Randy who deserved better than this double cross. The man that Dina had only hours ago denounced and told me to stay away from for a week.

I tapped the front of my Papsunized perfect white front teeth with my fingernail.

What the hell did I do now?

45

In front of me, the sea rises and swells. Behind me also, and to each side.

I have been at sea for forty days, a short time when placed against the rest of my life, but an eternity when serving under Captain Kasaba.

I left my home in sooty London a ragged and tattered boy and ran to the nearest boatyard, offering to serve the crown in any way they'd have me. And they put me here, aboard the H.M.S. Dowdy *and told me to mind my captain.*

When first I saw him, he stood back to the sun, with no face and no features showing, like the devil himself. In his two palms behind his back he held a whip. He held his authority.

As the boys and I went about our work, he stood above us, ready with the lash. Ready to drive his every whim home.

Captain Kasaba, the most feared sailor upon the seven seas, whose ship moves like a shark in the water.

And I have served these forty days and nights without

ever a word of complaint, without ever speaking before being spoken to. I have served and serviced my captain.

For it was on my first day that Captain Kasaba reached down from the featureless glare of the sun and grasped me hard by the jaw.

"See you come to my cabin tonight just after the first watch," he snarled.

And I did as I was told. I stole from my bunk and tapped lightly on his door.

As the door burst open, he again stood with his back to the only source of light. And again I saw no face. He stood with his legs spread wide, wearing the tatters of a sleeping gown, and he grabbed me again hard and pulled me into the cabin and pushed me against the wall. My eyes closed with the impact and I heard the sound of the cabin door slamming and then felt the rough surface of his face next to mine.

"You will do exactly as I tell ye," he growled and then told me some extraordinary things.

He left me aching and bloody as he satisfied himself with my body. I lay on the wooden floor with my eyes still closed tight out of terror and pain. Again, I felt him approach, this time as his rough face moved upon mine I felt his soft mouth cover my own. He pulled me into a moment's calm embrace and then let me fall again to the floor.

"Tell anyone of what happened here, and yer dead," he said and then, as I finally opened my eyes, sure that all was over, he swung open his cabin door.

Each day since then, the captain has come to me as I work on deck. Each night I have gone to him. He has taught me much with his whip and his body, much that, with a warmer soul, could bring to me great pleasure.

Today, the sky darkens to slate, the sea swells up into

mountains. And I am afraid of something more than my captain. In the distance, I can hear the thunder.

I do my work and keep my eyes trained down on the deck. Keep busy. I see the black boots of my captain before I know he's upon me. As he grasps my jaw and moves my head, I see a blood red sunset on the horizon.

"Tonight," he whispers with fetid breath, "we conclude your education."

There is electricity in the air. I am afraid.

The thunder is upon us. The watch calls down, "Ship!" And all eyes turn starboard. The captain takes this moment to pull me to him and run his lips on mine. "Tonight," he repeats as I fall forward toward those black boots.

"It be Captain Clean!" called the watch again, this time in more of a shriek. And panic was everywhere on the H.M.S. Dowdy.

All hands fell to weapons, but it was already, upon the sighting of the whiter-than-white flag of Captain Clean's ship, too late.

A cannonball across our deck brought about immediate devastation. And before we knew it, the ship of Captain Clean, most feared pirate on all the seven seas, was upon us.

The sky issued a torrent of rain, the storm swallowing us, just as the pirates rained down from the hull of their own ship. I stood my ground with only a bit of broken mast to defend me. And I looked up to see, through the haze of the day, the form of a man, who himself seemed to be the only source of light on the skyline.

This man, this blond angel, swung from ship to ship, holding a rope in one hand and a gleaming sword in the other.

His very presence seemed to seal the fate of the Dowdy. *Those sailors who did not lay down their arms were quickly dispatched by the pirates.*

Within the fray, I saw my captain turn to run, only to face down the bright angel, Captain Clean.

The two swords met at the top of the deck, but moved quickly and nimbly as my captain rushed down to the lower deck, toward his cabin. I followed them as best I could, hearing the sounds of desperate battle, the clang of metal, when the two were out of sight.

I knew why my captain raced to his cabin. I knew of the weapons hidden there and of the blackness in his heart.

Captain Clean fought bravely and well, his every action an example of fairness and fearlessness. But I knew that my captain had stored within his cabin enough gun-powder to sink this ship and that he would gladly sacrifice us all to kill the gleaming Clean.

A thrust from the one was returned by a parry, allow-ing me to get ahead of them and rush toward the captain's door. Seeing me, my captain swung wildly at me, claim-ing the flesh of my shoulder. I called out now in pain, as I'd never done before. And Captain Clean rushed to my side.

"Can I help you, lad?" he asked, his warm hands on my flowing wound.

"Stop him, Captain, or he'll blow us all sky high!" I called out, seeing the back of the dark captain reach the cabin door.

Captain Clean, in obvious discomfort at so ungentlemanly an act, did the necessary deed and pulled the dagger from his belt and stopped the evil man with a knife blow in the back.

He returned to my side. "You cannot die," he said, cradling me in his arms. "I won't permit it. You must sail with me across the ocean. And explore with me this world...."

It was hard for me to answer, as the power of exhaus-tion and fear had come over me. But I found the words as the last of my strength left my body. "Oh captain, take me with you. Take me from all of this, yes, please. . . ."

And the world swirled into darkness.

When next I awoke, it was in the sunlight, as I lay bandaged upon the deck of Captain Clean's own ship. As I rose slowly, I could see on the horizon, the smoldering remains of the H.M.S. Dowdy.

Captain Clean leaned down by my side. "Are you feeling any better, Laddie?" he asked.

"Much improved." I answered.

"And will you sail these seas with me? And be my special cabin boy?" he asked.

I nodded, wonderingly.

"Then when you're well enough, you must come on down to my cabin that I may teach you your duties," he said smiling.

I sat up fully then, leaning against his clean body. "I am well enough already," I answered him, "For you to show me your ways. . . ."

46

Feb 28

Dear Dina,

Don't hate me.

By the time you read this, I will have missed two or three sessions, depending on the mail, and you will already be certain that I am gone.

And I am, but not as thoughtlessly as you might think. Because it was nothing near casual, the way in which I winged out over the land to the sea.

Remember you were the hook of God that pulled me by the lip out of my ocean of despair.

This might overstate the case, but I cannot forget your kindness to me.

But how was I to know that when I got home again, to my shabby little home sweet home, so dear, so tattered but safe and warm after the horror of what had gone before — after I got back there, fully intent upon changing my clothes and getting on with my life, I found that I had a message from Lawrence. Upon seeing him again (and I was fully aware of my promise not to, I fully own my decision, for better or worse, of putting myself in emotional jeopardy) Lawrence insisted that we run away, first by plane and then for a cruise on one of the Love Boats, like they used to have on TV. I guess for him the Love Boat represents the height of romance.

So we're sailing to the South Seas under the full
and heavy moon.

I cannot tell you why I feel that I must go with
him. I cannot tell you what pulls me to his side. Maybe
it's something in the starch of his shirts, which I know
sounds daft at best, but there's a remoteness, a
purewhiteness about him that makes me want to curl up
next to him and sniff.

It surely isn't pure eroticism. As I might have at one
time hoped it would be. Back in the days when I
dreamed of seeing his organ, his dick, his cock, his
prick. Back when I hoped for, shall we say, largess?
When I dreamed that he was. . .penisissimo.

But I know better now. To my credit, I beautifully
weathered the fact that he is a dentist, given all the
fantasy careers I had given him. Did I ever tell you the
fantasy in which he was a pirate king and I the lowly
deckhand? I'm sure that I need go no further than that.

In my dreams, he always has the fullest, longest
golden hair. But, in this real world, I am content to
lightly touch the golden down that grows on his arm.

And I must say that I am entranced by his attraction
to me. As if his blue eys define me better than any
mirror ever has.

You see, I see us, Lawrence and me, as the eternal
lovers. Those on the Grecian Urn. Always kept apart.

Like Doug and Julie on *Days of Our Lives*.

The metaphor continues and unfolds:

In Rome, we are Romulus and Remus, two husky
guys who build the city of Rome with their own four
arms, with a song in their heart. With a vision that they
follow, together.

That's Lawrence and me. We are bigger than life,
when you look at our passion, at all that drives us
together and conspires to keep us apart.

Again, just like Doug and Julie on *Days of Our Lives.*

In the Middle Ages, we are the subject and object of Courtly Love. The knight and his squire. The knight in his perfectly clean and shining armor. The squire putting the palms of his hands together to make a ladder onto the horse, "Use me, use me to lift you higher," says the happy squire.

Yesterday, we were Oscar Wilde and his downfall, the boy for whom he went behind bars.

Today, we are Batman and Robin, the Dark Knight hiding a receding hairline under his cowl. Everybody knows that they are nothing but a pair of muscle-bound fags.

The point is: WE BELONG TOGETHER, in the words of Rickie Lee Jones.

I know that we are leaving Randy behind, and that he will be heartbroken and betrayed. And I know that my desertion will further alienate me from you, the dearest and most constant of friends. We also leave behind Lawrence's thriving practice.

But I know that I am moving forward by this action, that I am loosening the part of me that will feel instead of yearn. That I am, at last taking action.

Wildroot is riding high. Know this. There'll be action on the high seas tonight!

Much love,

Wildroot

P.S. Don't hate me.

47

Once years ago, I suddenly found myself getting very ill while over at a friend's house for supper. It was some sort of stomach virus, the kind that grips you instantly. A wave of nausea swept over me. Visibly, for my friend suggested that I had better excuse myself from the table and go and lie down for a bit.

I stood up, feeling that clammy coldness of the flu rush over me. Sparks of color flew across my eyes, all but blotting out the real world I was trying to see, as I nodded to all those gathered at the party and slowly made my way down the hall to the bedroom.

With relief, I allowed myself to topple over onto the bed, wishing myself into a healing coma. Instead, I felt the ripple upon ripple of a water bed below me. In my sickened state, I felt as if I had fallen into a tepid bowl of tapioca pudding.

I tried to stand up, but could not, I was caught within the wavelike motion of the water bed. And, to make matters worse, my hostess had, of course, not expected to have anyone use the bed, and so the heater had not been turned on, making it a particularly ghastly thing — a cold water bed.

I was now a buoy on the wide ocean, the wide rushing ocean of nausea. I felt my control of my whole digestive system raveling. The whole world was tossing and turning along with my stomach. I felt the color drain from my face and brought my hands up to eye level and saw that even they had taken on a greenish hue.

I saw the vein below my forefinger pounding out its rhythm thud-a-thud-a-thud, rolling and pounding on the bed.

And that did it.

I was never invited back there again.

The Love Boat, for me, was one huge water bed, with a kitchen and bedroom and bath all built right on top of it. There was never one moment in the next few weeks, in which I didn't feel some part of me churning in revolt against the quavering medium upon which we all rested. My traveling pain traveled as never before.

But, as I now sit again in Dina's warm office, realizing that perhaps it was the ocean waves that made me experience all my Love Boat adventures with hesitation, with a seven-second delay, at least I missed the end of winter. And returned one bleak Tuesday to watch the sun break through the clouds and realize that the thaw had come.

As I knocked on Dina's office door on this bleak Tuesday, right at six P.M., I prayed the prayer of the new believer that Dina would be inside.

Which she was, not even surprised to see me. And as I sat down by the table, waiting for her to return with the brewed tea, I glanced down at the calendar left open on the table, as if for me to see — my name written in every Tuesday at six P.M., a testament to her faith in me.

As I sat waiting, watching her head bob as she scooped honey into our mugs, I tried to pull together the information, the story of my days at sea:

In the car to the limo and the limo to the airport and the

plane to the Love Boat, Lawrence was unearthly quiet. At one point, midflight, I moved my knee to push it against his, only to find him moving his knee away from mine. Although he gave me his toasted almonds without my even asking, I was not at all sure that all was right.

I was altogether sure that nothing much was going right by the time I got my first look at the Love Boat. For I had the idea of the television series in mind, that Gopher and everybody else would be on deck to greet us, and that faded celebrities would all be on board to frolic with us and work out their marital woes as we worked out ours.

This did not appear to be the case, as both the crew and the other passengers were more than double our age.

Suffice it to say that the line moved slowly, what with ancient porters taking the luggage from the ancient passengers, whose names were checked off the passenger lists by an ancient crew.

But, when we reached the top of the gangplank and actually stepped onto the boat, I was altogether sure that this just was not going to work out right. For there, just to the left of the captain's slouched shoulder, was a poster for our voyage's entertainment, "The Seven Ages of Elvis." And beneath the poster surrounded by his own name spelled out in glitter-covered letters, was a grotesque black-and-white glossy of Benny Roshomon's face.

I say grotesque in that the photographer had taken it in such a way as to make Benny look old, evil, shriveled, and overweight all at once.

I was later to learn that Thallassa herself had taken the photo.

I turned to Lawrence with terror in my eyes. What if he remembered Benny? But then I remembered that Lawrence had never met Benny, but had only been tailed by him, and that it was Randy who knew Benny, had gone to exercise class with him. Now, if only Randy had never told Lawrence about Benny.

Lawrence followed my eyes to the poster. "I saw him on New Year's Eve," he said with some excitement. "It's one of the reasons I booked this particular cruise."

So far so good.

I followed Lawrence who followed the ancient porter down to our room. We carried our own luggage, in that neither of us had the heart to simply follow along and watch him carry it.

The cabin bore out my fear that this was not a Love Boat at all, but was instead a floating Motel 6.

Everything was aqua and pink, like one large bathroom. The furniture was fifties modern, everything low and flat, like living on a mesa.

"Nice room," said Lawrence over my shoulder. We were cooked.

But the room, I had to admit, did have one really nice feature — one huge bed.

I sat down on the bed and patted the patch of bed next to mine. Lawrence went into the bathroom and closed the door. Locked it. Turned on the water for a long time so that I couldn't hear what he was doing.

When he came back out of the bathroom, he found me lying prostrate across the bed, dressed in a diaphanous silk nightshirt. I had left it open to the navel.

Lawrence took one look at me and backed part way back into the bathroom. "I can't," he said quietly. His face was very pale.

I gathered my garment around me, and pulled it tight. "Sit down," I ordered. I figured that we might as well get this over with quickly.

And it didn't take long to get the story out of him. That he had left Randy crying when he told him about me and about the cruise. When I asked, he assured me that he hadn't mentioned my name. I was only "Someone Else."

Lawrence had GUILT written all over his face. I knew how he felt, but I also knew that I'd come too far to give up on him now.

But I let it go for the moment, and we, talking and walking together, went back up on the deck — after I'd slipped my pants and shirt back on — and watched the Love Boat push off.

In the hours that followed, we each signed up for shuffleboard and we walked around the ship, finding the pool, the various decks, the lounge, and the dining room.

We then spent an uneventful dinner chatting with our tablemates, a couple from Des Moines.

After dinner, horror began to follow horror as Lawrence suggested that we go to see Benny perform. I would have immediately refused, but it was the first and only thing so far that he seemed eager to do.

So I adjusted my tie with a sigh and we went to the ship's nightclub.

As we neared the door to the lounge, I caught sight of Thallassa on the withered arm of our ship's captain. An instantaneous coughing fit kept me out of her sight line. And then we were inside the door.

I flatly and without excuse refused to sit at the front-row table that Lawrence pointed out and instead insisted that we sit toward the back of the room. All of this was in spite of the fact that Benny's maiden performance was being lightly attended, perhaps due to its ten P.M. curtain time.

"I might want to slip out," I hissed at Lawrence.

"You won't want to leave," he answered. "I told you. I saw him on New Year's Eve. He's great."

And so we sat down to wait for the show to begin. I kept my eye out for Thallassa, but as she walked past us, with the captain still being more than half supported by her strong left arm, she was much too busy feigning amusement at whatever bon mot he had just uttered to ever look at me.

Finally the lights dimmed. The audience's shrill chatter quieted to rapt attention.

This time, I watched Benny's show, and was surprised to find that he had actually mined his material for some dramatic impact. That he had used his wits and creativity here as he had for "Christmas in Paris." Here was Elvis the boy, with his lower lip thrust out, and then Elvis the young man, with his pelvis swaying in the breeze. And on and on, until the theme from *2001* pounded out and we saw Elvis' Las Vegas years, fat and old before his time. And, somehow, Benny had done it all, had aged with this man, had honestly presented Elvis alpha to omega.

As the strains of "My Way" began — and Benny, with all his show-biz savvy had brought prerecorded music and was not dependent upon the ship's decrepit dance band — Benny began to walk out into the audience.

This was meant to be the penultimate moment, the final benediction that left no one dry-eyed as Elvis died again, as if for our sins. But what this did was bring us eye to eye.

I had known in my bones that this moment would happen. That Benny and I would end up eye-to-eye. But what I should also have known is that (1) Benny was too much of a professional ham ever to share his spotlight with me, even in this shock of seeing me in the last place he'd ever thought of finding me; (2) my eyes would be pumping out all the information I needed to convey, with messages like, "Give me a break, huh?" and "Yeah, I finally landed the guy"; and (3) Benny would laugh down to the bottom of his heart seeing me here and finding me in this mess.

In that moment, without a word exchanged, Benny, in his padded fat Elvis white jumpsuit and cape, with his arms outstretched and upraised, forgave me every rotten thing I'd ever done to him. And I forgave Benny. We were friends again.

When the time for applause came, I clapped harder than anyone else.

"I told you that you'd like it," Lawrence said to me.

And when a bucket of cold champagne came over to our table a few minutes later, I knew where it had come from and what it meant.

Whether it was because the tension that had built within my body had ended at my moment of Elvis Blessing, or not, things seemed to be better between Lawrence and me after that.

We popped the cork and I toasted him and his good taste at having booked this voyage. I told him how brilliant the show had been, almost as if he himself had written it, instead of just buying the tickets. I flashed my eyes in his direction.

We drank our champagne shamelessly. Toasting loudly and staring deeply into each other's eyes. It was domestic champagne, a California sparkling wine, but it was the best they had on board and we liked it just fine. In fact, when we finished that bottle, Lawrence ordered another.

And I told him of his valor in booking this voyage and of making this the first day of the rest of our lives — together. And every time I saw the ghost of Randy rise vapidly between us, I removed my foot from my shoe and played my toes lightly up and down Lawrence's leg, just as I had once shamelessly done to Randy. In fact, I even nestled my foot in Lawrence's crotch, and felt it grow hard beneath me. Again, my eyes flashed shamelessly.

By now what few oldsters who had remained for a drink after the show had gone on to bed, making me really brazen. My hands slipped under the tiny table, to play in the fields of Lawrence's thighs. And they replaced my foot over his crotch. Again I hissed. For a third time my eyes flashed. And I rose to my feet, my arms suddenly akimbo.

We left the lounge at this point and walked closely packed and touching along the lower deck to our cabin. The moon was full and beginning to set. The salt air was overwhelmingly seductive.

I followed Lawrence down the narrow corridor to our cabin and brushed my body against his as he unlocked our door and stepped aside for me to pass.

This time I didn't bother with my nightgown. This time I didn't let him anywhere near the bathroom door.

I was on him like a duck on a June bug.

We rolled over and over on the too soft bed, the lower person always sinking below the level of breathing, as his head went down down down into the old mattress. I undressed my man as we thrust and rolled. Easing his cotton clothing from his body. He has a look of bewilderment on his face, and a flush of drunken joy.

Our rhythm matched and we stepped up our pace.Saliva covered our bodies. I reached my hand under my side of the mattress and brought forth my consummation kit. All the jells and condoms were nestled within. Something for everyone.

I was lubricated before Lawrence knew what was happening, as I thought it best to move quickly while the wine and the sea and my akimbo action were still strongly in effect.

And Lawrence, I must say, responded beautifully. I unwrapped the condom and slipped it over his erect organ. His cock bounced in happy rhythm as he approached my castle gate. And we both were just so happy.

Then it hit me.

The traveling pain. It swelled up my left arm and drove hard across my shoulders. And I heard Randy call my name, "Wildroot, Wildroot, why are you doing this to me?" And

I swear that for a moment I could see him, Randy, standing there, looking at me, calling my name, just like Auntie Em calls out "Dorothy, Dorothy," when Dorothy sees her in the Wicked Witch's crystal ball.

A shudder, a jolt, a bolt of pain went through me. And in this instant, Lawrence breached my castle gate.

I felt the pain from all sides, the whoosh of its movement, like being run over by a truck. I screamed out in agony. Lawrence, misunderstanding the reason for my shout, only thrust harder.

And then there was a humming in the air that came from nowhere, a whoosh and a thud and a bright white light. I was having a religious experience.

The traveling pain, in a ball of guilt and fear, moved through me, through my digestive track and out of my body.

Moved out of my body and into Lawrence's by virtue of our joined position. I heard him scream in pain, such pain, as I felt it leave my body.

And from that moment, Lawrence was forever rubbing his body, whether it be his temple or his stomach, or the cock that was the seat of the problem, the entry point.

He was rubbing and screaming when he suddenly pulled out of my body. And he continued rubbing and screaming as I called the ship's doctor and as Lawrence was taken off the boat the next day on a stretcher to some foreign hospital.

What was I to tell him? That I'd given him a case of an unimaginably potent venereal disease? He'd never believe it, anyway.

And so I stayed on the voyage. It was paid for, after all, and left Lawrence in his clean white hospital bed, after making sure that all was well with him. I knew the doctors would find nothing wrong with him and that he'd grow accustomed to the traveling pain in time.

I wired Randy from the next port of call. "Come and

get your lover," the wire said, along with the name of
the hospital. I signed the wire, "A Friend," and really
meant it.

For the next few days that followed, I hung by the side of
the deck, looking out to sea. There were moments in which
I considered slipping over the deck, like Hart Crane, who
had sunk himself in these waters.

But I never let my feet begin the dive. I clung to the
rail and thought my thoughts in salt air.

About the fourth day of doing this, I suddenly was aware
of Benny at my side. "I thought I'd give the two of you a
little time alone before I said hello," he said.

I told him Lawrence was gone and then told him the
whole story. And that put roses in his cheeks and gave him
a good laugh. He put his arm around me then and we
walked in out of the fresh air.

As we talked then and regained our mutual knowledge
and affection, I told him how good I had really found his
show to be. But I told him of some changes I'd make in the
blocking and the stage.

Without even answering me directly, he stood up and
ran from the room, returning with Thallassa and the captain. Thallassa greeted me in a little too friendly a fashion.
But she was pleased to see me, and that was obvious. "How
much would you charge us?" she asked in her German
accent.

I told her I didn't know what she was talking about.

"To restage the show," she told me.

I was amazed, overwhelmed. To finally get to design
a stage show. I'd do it for free, I wanted to say. And then
I quoted her the price of the tow-truck driver for whom I'd
written the bad check.

"Done!" Thallassa answered, squeezing my lips in her

clawlike hand. And she and the captain went off to promenade.

Benny and I set to work. Planning, scheming. A red spotlight here, a bit of gunpowder there and we were ready for his performance on the last night of the cruise.

This time the room was packed with the passengers who'd gotten used to vacation hours. This time the room was abubble with excited chatter as everyone awaited "The Seven Ages of Elvis."

I stood in the back of the room. The drumroll opened the show and Benny was there doing his ingenious "faux Elvis." And for the next few minutes, the King was back again. We laughed, we cried and the staging was FUCKING FANTASTIC. Most especially the fireworks that climaxed "My Way."

And don't think for a moment that this was easy, getting everything we needed for this show in the shoddy ports of call we had available to us. Hideous little islands on which everything seemed prefab, everything from K-mart. But I decorated as I've never decorated before, with staging flowing from my fingertips. Mantis, eat your fucking damned heart out.

After Elvis had lost his forty pounds of padding and reverted back to Benny, we each sat, freshly showered on my huge soft bed. More than once, I considered the consummation kit, but, in the end, we rejoiced together and remembered old times and looked ahead to the future, each knowing that the other was moving off alone to another place.

As the evening ended and exhaustion washed over us, Benny and I embraced, fully and deeply and kissed each other even more deeply, for we had a true true feeling for each other that transcended a given name.

The next morning, as the ship docked, I had my bags
packed and was ready to go. Benny saw me off then, telling
me so much at once. Where to write him at his P.O. box.
That he was going out on the ship again immediately, or
he'd come with me part of the way. That he'd pay me a
percentage of his take with the show, as I'd improved it so
much. And that he'd miss me.

I believed him about all of it but the money.

And as I walked down the gangplank, I looked back to
see Benny waving a white handkerchief at me, and screaming "Good-bye!" at the top of his lungs.

As soon as I got to the airport, I cashed in Lawrence's
ticket for spending money. I paid the cab who'd driven me
there and bought myself a dinner.

Then I flew home, asking for extra toasted almonds on
the flight and took a taxi to my apartment.

All was just as I had left it, although I felt that years
had passed in only days. I felt that my ghosts, like Scrooge's
had gotten me through it all in moments. . . .

As I sit here now in Dina's office, at Dina's table, the familiar
washes over me. Dina brings two mugs of steaming tea and
sits across from me. She looks at me without challenge. She
knows that I have changed.

No more Pain.

And we begin the session. She's holding back not sure
how to begin. A little angry at what I've done, but also glad
to see me back, safe.

I look at Dina and her image shifts. She is Mother Seton
and the Queen of Night. Hecate and then Lillian Hellman.
But I keep looking, past the shift and, at last, she is Dina
again.

"Wildroot," she says, reaching her hand across the table
to me.

My hand reaches back, Sistine-like, not touching. "Dina," I say, not sure of what I should be saying.

"Dina," I say again, my hand breaching the gap, reaching her own and touching, "Dina, call me Wyatt."

Epilogue

All of which brings us pretty much up to date. Pretty much right up to the second, in fact.

Except for where I find myself right now, which is the blessed event, not which was never sought after or looked at, but which cannot surprise the sensitive reader.

I am at the wedding of Orly and Pixie.

And for once I am not crashing, I am an invited guest. Friend of the bride and friend of the groom. The one who brought them together.

And, although perhaps there are those who would say, myself among them on a bad day, that I should be giving the bride away or at least a groomsman, I am truly grateful and truly happy just to be in attendance.

It was not easy to reestablish contact with Pixie. Instead of howling by her door or waiting in a sulk for her to call me, I just called one day soon after I got off the damned boat and I asked her to coffee. I said I wanted to clear the air. And that I was sorry at the loss of the friendship we'd shared for years.

We had small talk with our coffee. And afterward, on one of those first sunny days that lure you into the belief that spring is here forever and not just for the afternoon, we sat out on a stone fence and finally had ourselves a talk. We could see our breath in the air, but the sun was hot on our faces.

I had to tell her that what happened between her brother and me was as precious to me as what had happened to me with her. That both were explorations — sexual explorations — between young people who were left to figure things out for themselves by parents who were too embarrassed to get involved. What had happened for Rollo was a quick dip into a different pool, and nothing else, nothing more than that, but for me it triggered a deeper and constant longing. Therefore, I couldn't really bring myself to be sorry about what had happened between us, only that he, once he called off the sex, had to call off the friendship, too — something that Pixie and I had never done.

And after a while I think she began to understand a bit and I could slowly feel the bridges mending.

It was a few days after this that I got my invitation in the mail and sent my tuxedo out to the cleaners, although I had to rent the shoes.

And Pixie did more in the next few days to heal our fractured love. For Orly suddenly called me on the phone to offer me a job with Kasaba Brothers Men's Clothing, doing the window displays for all the stores. The work is not challenging, what with just the guy dummies in their blue suits and contrasting pocket squares and ties, but the money is steady and, for me, it is big bucks.

New car time.

And, no, I never did follow Dina's advice completely. I never did tell Pixie about my lunch with Orly. Faith and trust, I figure, only extend so far. . . .

And best of all, is the fact that, in my new work, I never have to deal with Orly, who stands now in the front of this church, festooned as it is in pink and white. He stands up at the altar, an Aztec deity, waiting for his bride. And I'll never have to try and look him in the eye — a point, I believe, that is of mutual relief. Instead, I am working daily and very closely with his brother, Ken Kasaba, who stands not quite so tall as his brother but has a dimple in his gorgeous little chin. He is sitting beside me now in the fourth row back at this wedding, on the aisle and is applying unmistakable pressure on my thigh with his wide-spread knee. It will be fun finding out if he means it.

And Mendelssohn's traditional wedding march is playing. And we all rise to turn and watch the bride glide down the aisle. She is wearing a soft light pink dress and is as radiant as the first delicate spring flowers that are woven in her hair.

And here I am totally happy, surrounded in the light of wedding candles and the perfume of the flowers, as my dear friend, my sister winks at me as she passes. And I must say, except for that huge ribbon that she's selected to wrap her midriff, and except for the flowers that she carries from the florist that I could have arranged so much better, she really really really does look almost good enough to eat.

*   *   *   *

Duncan Campbell Scott writes many different stories
and articles under various names. This is his first novel.
Like Wildroot, he is trying to make some sense out
of his life.